A SMALL TOWN HOLIDAY ROMANCE

If You Give a GRUMP a Holiday WISHLIST

ANN EINERSON

Paperback ISBN: 978-1-960325-06-8

Cover Design by Sarah, Okay Creations

Edited by Caroline Palmier, Love and Edits; Jovana Shirley, Unforeseen Editing; and Brooke Crites, Proofreading by Brooke

For those who wished for a grumpy, hot as coal billionaire for Christmas this year, Jack Sinclair is my gift to you.

AUTHOR'S NOTE

Hey Reader!

Thank you for picking up *If You Give a Grump a Holiday Wishlist*. The holiday season is my favorite, so naturally I had to write a sweet and spicy romance centered around this magical time of year.

If You Give a Grump a Holiday Wishlist is a small town, fake dating, one bed, spicy workplace holiday romance. It's a lighthearted story meant to get you in the holiday spirit. *If You Give a Grump a Holiday Wishlist* contains explicit sexual content, profanity, and mention of absentee parents. Reading is meant to be your happy place—choose yourself, your needs, and your happiness first!

Xoxo,

Ann Einerson

PLAYLIST

9 to 5 - Dolly Parton

Like It's Christmas - Jonas Brothers

You're On Your Own Kid - Taylor Swift

Maine - Noah Kahan

All I Want For Christmas Is You - Mariah Carey

Like Real People Do - Hozier

Christmas Tree Farm - Taylor Swift

Mistletoe - Justin Bieber

If you give a grump a holiday wishlist, you might be tempted to invite him home for the holidays. And if you invite him home for the holidays, he'll pretend to be your boyfriend. He'll want to sleep in the same bed so everyone thinks that you're a couple, and then he'll ask you for a kiss under the mistletoe so he knows what you taste like...

PROLOGUE

JACK

THREE YEARS AGO

"TELL ME THAT WAS THE last interview for the day." I rub my temples to ward off an oncoming headache.

"Sorry, but no. You have one more," Valentine says as she waltzes into my office.

As head of HR, she's taken it upon herself to find me an assistant. I built Sinclair Group from the ground up and have been doing just fine without one. However, Valentine says I'm unapproachable and most of my staff is intimidated by me. She thinks an assistant can act as a liaison to improve my rapport with employees and free me up for more pressing issues. I disagree, but she's adamant about this particular matter.

"Stop being dramatic. It's not like I'm forcing you to get a root canal or sit through a four-hour board meeting," she says with a hint of amusement. "You should be thanking me for wanting to make your life easier."

"I would rather watch paint dry for an hour than sit through another interview like my last one," I say.

"Well, you're in luck because I saved the best for last."

"Who is it?"

"Her name is Presley Stafford. She's worked for Franklin Holdings in Tribeca as an assistant to a group of mid-level managers for the past two years. During her phone interview, she mentioned that she's looking for a new challenge, and all her references gave her glowing recommendations."

"Where did she go to college?"

Valentine doesn't respond right away, leaving me suspicious. "She didn't go to college," she says hesitantly.

"Come again?"

"She moved to New York right out of high school and has worked at Franklin Holdings since."

I squeeze the bridge of my nose between my fingers, praying for patience. "I specifically asked that we make a college degree a requirement for this position," I remind Valentine.

"It was a requirement, but Ms. Stafford's cover letter was rather convincing, and I couldn't pass up the opportunity to speak with her. She's tenacious, driven, and bold, and something tells me you'll get along swimmingly." Valentine stands her ground.

I should tell her to cancel the interview since Ms. Stafford doesn't meet the qualifications for the position. However, she won't rest until I hire someone, so I might as well humor her.

IF YOU GIVE A GRUMP A HOLIDAY WISHLIST

"Fine, but if this interview goes south, I want you to wait a week before bringing in another round of candidates."

"Whatever you say," Valentine says dismissively. "I'll send Presley in when she arrives." She steps out into the hall.

I lean back in my chair and close my eyes. Finally, I have some peace and quiet. It's not an easy task running a multibillion-dollar investment firm. There's a constant weight on my shoulders to do better and work harder. While it can get lonely, I don't have much free time to dwell on it.

I'm interrupted by heels clapping against the vinyl floor outside my office. It's probably a legal intern dropping off another contract for me to review.

"Christ, is it too much to ask for five minutes of—"

I stop short when I glance up to see a gorgeous woman standing in the doorway. She looks young, probably in her early twenties, and has a stunning hourglass figure. Her brown hair is pulled back into a high ponytail, and her piercing blue eyes shoot me a curious glance. She's wearing a black pencil skirt, a white turtleneck, and a fitted blazer, completing the sophisticated look with black pumps.

Based on my reaction, you'd think this was the first beautiful woman I've ever met. Her lips are painted cherry red, tempting me to stroke her jawline while smudging her lipstick with my thumb. I'm stunned speechless, unsure how to interrupt my unexpected visceral reaction. I'm so focused on my thoughts that I barely register she's speaking to me.

"If you're always this pleasant, I'm surprised there isn't a line out the door of eager applicants begging to fill the position," she jokes.

I blink rapidly, caught off guard by her bold remark.

"Who are you?" My voice comes out cold, and she frowns at my clipped response.

"I'm Presley Stafford. I'm here for my interview. Valentine sent me in," she states with confidence. "It's a pleasure to meet you, Mr. Sinclair."

I like hearing her say my name.

She extends her hand, and I reciprocate with a handshake. I notice her hand is soft, a striking contrast from her firm grip. The smell of vanilla and roses infiltrates my nose, and I resist the urge to pull her closer. I remind myself that she's here for business and I need maintain a professional demeanor.

"Take a seat." I motion to the chair opposite my desk and settle into mine on the other side. "Tell me, Ms. Stafford, why do you want to work at Sinclair Group?"

"I'm looking for a new challenge," she starts. "Valentine mentioned that it was important to you that your new assistant has a college degree. While I don't have one, I believe my real-world experience is equally as valuable. My knowledge of the investment industry is extensive, and I'm committed to surpassing your expectations, if given the chance. While I'm happy to make your coffee and take meticulous meeting notes, I won't hesitate to voice my opinion if it can bring value to a discussion." She straightens up in her chair. "I'll be frank, Mr. Sinclair. You have an impressive track record, and you need someone of equal caliber working by your side."

"You're my ninth interview today," I inform her. "What makes you think I haven't already extended a job offer to someone else and am merely interviewing you as a formality?"

She lets out a soft laugh. "You don't strike me as someone who would give that kind of courtesy. You're a busy man, and

4

if you'd already filled the position, I would have gotten a call informing me that my interview had been canceled."

I drum my fingers on my desk, contemplating how to respond. Truth be told, when Presley walked through the door, part of me hoped I'd be able to quickly dismiss her as a qualified candidate. She might be too young for me, but it wouldn't have stopped me from asking her to dinner.

Unfortunately, I have to put the brakes on that particular fantasy, considering Valentine was right—Presley Stafford would be perfect for this position. The problem is figuring out how to maintain a professional working relationship with a woman I'm tempted to bend over my desk.

The rest of the interview goes by in a blur, and before I know it our hour is up.

"Thank you for your time, Ms. Stafford. My team will be in touch." I stand up to escort her out—a gesture I haven't extended to any of the other candidates.

"I look forward to working with you, Mr. Sinclair," Presley says confidently before striding out the door.

If she were anyone else, her bold assumption that I'm going to offer her the position would be off-putting. However, I'm impressed by her tenacity and determination, placing her far ahead of the other applicants despite her lack of a higher education. There's no denying that hiring her would be a smart business decision, but it's going to test my self-control. I'll have to keep things strictly professional, starting by verbally addressing her only as Ms. Stafford during our conversations.

ONE YEAR AGO

I storm down the hall after another unproductive meeting with Mr. Wescott and his team. The bastard is playing hardball, and if his investment firm wasn't the best on the West Coast, I wouldn't be so keen on acquiring his company. At this rate, it could be another year before the deal is complete.

On my way back to my office, I stop by Presley's empty desk when a piece of red paper catches my eye. Her work station is usually spotless so I can't help but question what it's doing there. While I acknowledge that I shouldn't invade her privacy, my curiosity gets the best of me. I glance around to make sure I'm alone before leaning over to get a quick peek.

Presley's Holiday Wishlist

1. ~~Build a snowman~~
2. ~~Make a gingerbread house~~
3. ~~Holiday movie marathon + hot chocolate~~
4. ~~Decorate a real Christmas tree~~
5. ~~Write a letter to Santa~~
6. *Kiss under the mistletoe*

It appears to be a list of activities Presley completed while she was away for the holidays. Her absence for the three days she was out of the office left an unmistakable void.

My jaw clenches when I reach the final item on the list.

Kiss under the mistletoe? What the fuck?

If it's not crossed off, does that mean it didn't happen? I emit a low growl, and a wave of possessiveness washes over me just thinking about another man touching her. I wonder if she's seeing anyone. Who am I kidding? She's a gorgeous, young woman, living in the city; of course she's dating. Regardless, it shouldn't matter to me. I have no business caring about her personal life, considering I'm her boss and I have done everything to ensure our relationship has remained strictly professional during the last two years.

"Mr. Sinclair, what are you doing?"

My head snaps up to see Presley walking toward me.

"Shit," I mutter under my breath.

I hastily shove her wishlist under the pile of papers on her desk, pretending to search through the stack.

"I need the Clarkston Fundamentals report. Where is it?" My voice comes out cold and demanding. I internally cringe at my tone but don't apologize.

"It's right here." She slaps down a bound copy of the report onto her desk. "I skipped lunch to make sure you had it in time for your meeting this afternoon. Did you need anything else?" she asks briskly.

I admit I enjoy provoking her so I can witness her sassy side. Despite maintaining a professional relationship, I appreciate her willingness to speak her mind regardless of my role as CEO.

"That'll be all." I grab the report, ready to rush back to my office.

"Mr. Sinclair, I think you're forgetting something." Presley's melodic voice has me spinning around without pause.

She folds her arms across her chest, fixing me with a frosty glare. God, why does she have to be so cute when she's mad?

"And what might that be, Ms. Stafford?"

"Your manners." She nods to the report in my hand.

I suppress a smile of admiration at her insistence on being treated with the utmost respect.

"Thank you for putting this together so quickly, Ms. Stafford." I gesture to the report. "It's very much appreciated," I say with sincerity.

"You're very welcome." She flashes me a grin, making me think of all the wicked things I could do with that pretty little mouth of hers. "Before you go, I wanted to let you know that I'm taking off two weeks of work next December. My mom was disappointed that I had to cut my visit short this year, and I won't let that happen again. I'll remind you as it gets closer, but I just wanted to let you know well in advance."

I don't like the idea of her being gone for that long. It doesn't matter, considering it's a year away. Anything could happen between now and then.

"We can discuss it when it gets closer," I say tersely. "For now, get back to work."

"That's fine. I'm putting it on your calendar since I wouldn't want you to forget," she says with a smirk.

"Okay." I give her a curt nod before walking away.

Since Presley Stafford stepped into my office for the first time, she's never been far from my mind. I can only hope that someday, her presence won't have such a profound effect on me. She's become an indispensable part of my team at Sinclair Group and I don't want to do anything to jeopardize our working relationship. No matter how tempted I might be to cross that line.

1

PRESLEY

PRESENT DAY

WHO THE HELL DOES JACK SINCLAIR think he is?

I narrow my eyes at the email that just hit my inbox.

Ms. Stafford,
The Wescott acquisition has been finalized. We're meeting with Mr.
Wescott and his team on Friday to plan the transition before the new
year. He and his associates will be calling in remotely. Block out our
calendar for tomorrow so we can prepare.
Your boss,
Jack Sinclair

It's official—I hate him. He knows damn well that today was meant to be my last day of work until after the holidays.

He has no right to demand that I delay my well-earned time off. The deal is complete, and these meetings can wait until January. I guarantee I'm not the only one who thinks so. Just because Jack Sinclair doesn't have a life outside of work doesn't mean the rest of us don't.

I can't help but scoff when I see his signature. I'll never understand why he insists on signing every email with "your boss." How could I possibly forget that I work for a moody, high-strung asshole who has no regard for anyone but himself.

My phone chimes, letting me know my rideshare is waiting downstairs. I've already had to cancel my pickup twice because Jack is adamant that I be in the office when he is.

The handle of my suitcase peeks out from the side of my desk—another reminder that I was supposed to leave for the airport hours ago. Even if it wasn't rush hour, there's no way I'd catch my flight. I let out an exasperated sigh and cancel my ride for the third time today.

I wonder what the chances are my mother would let it slide if I couldn't make it home for Christmas. *Zero.* She'd drag the whole family to New York before she would let me skip out on spending the holidays with them in Aspen Grove. Plus it wouldn't be the same if they came here.

I frown down at the piece of paper on my desk. Every year since I was a kid, I've made a list of things to do during the holiday season. Some are long-standing traditions, and others are new things I want to try. Regardless of my mother's wishes, I can't help but wonder how many I could check off if I stayed in the city.

Presley's Holiday Wishlist

1. *Go ice skating*
2. *Visit the local Christmas market*
3. *Try a roasted chestnut*
4. *Write a letter to Santa*
5. *Make a gingerbread house*
6. *Holiday movie marathon + hot chocolate*
7. *Decorate a real Christmas tree*
8. ~~*Kiss under the mistletoe*~~

It would be a pain in the ass to haul a tree up to my fifth-floor apartment, and making a gingerbread house wouldn't be any fun without it being a competition with my brothers.

I crossed out "kiss under the mistletoe" because there's no chance of that happening, considering I haven't even been on a date in over two years. The last guy I dated, Brennan, broke up with me after a month because he said I was a workaholic. Apparently he needed to be with someone who was willing to put their relationship first.

It's not my fault Jack Sinclair doesn't understand the term *work-life balance*. He's been the bane of my existence since I started working here three years ago. God, even his name is pretentious. It's like his parents wanted him to be a control freak with a stick shoved up his ass.

He might be a temperamental bastard, but there is no denying his brilliance. He's a thirty-two-year-old billionaire CEO of a global investment firm that he single-handedly built from the ground up. His credentials are impressive as hell, and

I've learned a lot from working for him, but it comes with a multitude of challenges.

At six-two, he commands every room he walks into, and it doesn't hurt that he's sexy as hell either. He has honey-colored eyes, black hair that's always perfectly styled in a crew cut, and a rugged jawline that accentuates his features. Did I mention he looks utterly irresistible in a three-piece charcoal-gray suit? I always assumed that the stereotypical hot billionaire type was only reserved for romance novels, but Jack is proof that's not true.

If only he had a personality to match his appearance.

"Ms. Stafford," he calls from his office, like he can sense that I'm ignoring his email.

He's never embraced the concept of sending me a chat or calling me on the phone like a civil human being. No, he prefers to bark orders at me like a dog meant to heel. Thank God everyone else has left for the night.

I fold up my wishlist and tuck it into my pocket before marching into his office.

"You shouted, Mr. Sinclair?" I deadpan.

"Why haven't you responded to my email?"

"You mean the one you sent two minutes ago?"

"Yes." He doesn't bother looking up from his computer. "Block out my calendar for tomorrow so we can prepare for our meetings with Mr. Wescott's team."

"Unfortunately, I'm not available." I square my shoulders, bracing for his imminent outburst.

"Why the hell not? It's your job." He stops typing in favor of glaring across at me.

I'm glad I finally have his undivided attention.

"Because I'll be out of town. It's been on your calendar since January, and I've sent you monthly reminders so you wouldn't forget that I'd be out of the office during the last two weeks of the year."

"Reschedule," he demands.

God, the nerve of this man. I clench my fists, trying to suppress my anger before I say something that'll get me fired. You'd think after three years of hard work and dedication I would have earned an ounce of his respect, but apparently not.

"Let me get this straight," I start. "You're asking me to change my holiday plans with my family?" There's a hint of disdain in my tone. "Mr. Sinclair, I'm not canceling my vacation."

"This is the biggest acquisition in the company's history. I need you here."

"Well, I'm unavailable." I stand firm, refusing to give in. "As of yesterday, Wescott International is officially a subsidiary of Sinclair Group. Whatever you need my help with can wait until the new year. I'm sorry my personal life is getting in the way of you doing business, but I haven't taken a single day off since last December, all so that I could go home for Christmas, and you're not taking that away from me. I've already missed my flight, and my poor mother will be in a frenzy when she finds out."

"Where does your family live?"

"Aspen Grove, Maine?" I say it like a question, not sure why he cares.

I expect him to call me insubordinate and tell me to pack my things and never come back. Instead, Jack picks up his phone and begins furiously typing away, ignoring me again.

Just as I'm ready to walk out of his office, he glances up. "Finish whatever you're working on. We're leaving in ten minutes," he instructs. "I'm assuming you have your suitcase here if you were planning to go straight to the airport?"

"Um...yes," I say hesitantly. "I'm confused. Where are we going?"

"Aspen Grove. Clearly you weren't taught how to compromise, so I'll just have to come with you. We'll work from the hotel."

I burst into laughter, not able to stop myself. Just when I think Jack might have finally grown a sense of humor, the scowl on his face tells me that's not the case.

He's not kidding.

"You can't be serious." I begin nervously pacing.

"I don't waste my time with jokes, Ms. Stafford. We're at an impasse, and I've provided a viable solution. I fail to see the problem."

"You can't just invite yourself to come home with me."

"Why not? I'll stay at a hotel, and you can help me during the days and spend the evenings with your family. It's only for a few days, and once I head back to the city, you can have until the new year to yourself."

I guess that might work.

Wait... Why am I entertaining this idea? The last thing I want to do is to bring my overbearing boss back to Aspen Grove.

"What if I set up a conference call for us tomorrow? That way you can stay here."

"No."

"Why not?" I practically screech.

"You know how I feel about you working remotely. It's not nearly as efficient as being in the same room together, and it's far too distracting."

I did know how he felt about remote work, but I hoped he'd cave because of the circumstances. If I can't get out of this, I'm damn well going to make it work in my favor.

"I have conditions."

"I'd expect nothing less." Jack laces his hands behind his head, leaning back in his chair. "What are they?"

"I want a thirty-percent raise, effective immediately. I've more than earned it," I state with more confidence than I feel. "And I don't want my family to know you're my boss; it'll only complicate things."

The last thing I need is for my mother to go postal on the man who makes my work life a living hell.

"You drive a hard bargain, Ms. Stafford. Anything else?"

I'm about to say no when a harebrained idea pops into my head.

"Yes. I want you to help me with my holiday wishlist."

I'm going to regret this.

No, scratch that. I already do.

"I'm sorry, your *what?*" he asks, confusion written all over his face.

I pull the list from my pocket and place it on Jack's desk.

"My holiday wishlist. Every year, I make a list of things I want to do while I'm visiting home that help me get in the holiday spirit."

He hesitantly unfolds the paper, his eyes widening with every line he reads.

"A letter to Santa Claus. Really, Ms. Stafford? Are you a child?"

"It's a tradition." I shrug. "I've written him a letter every year since I was a kid."

His impassive expression makes me think he's not impressed with my answer, and his lips form a thin line when he gets to the end of the list.

"It looks like you already have someone to help you this year," he says flatly.

"What are you talking about?"

He slides the letter in my direction, pointing to *kiss under the mistletoe.*

"It's been crossed off, and I know for a fact *that* particular activity requires two people to participate," he states.

Oh my god.

My cheeks flush with embarrassment. How could I have forgotten that was on there?

"I crossed that item off because it's not something I can do this year." I keep my voice steady.

"And why is that?"

"If you haven't noticed, Mr. Sinclair, I don't exactly have a lot of free time to date," I say in a snarky tone. "And I'm not the kind of person who goes around kissing strangers."

A brief glimpse of relief crosses his face, but it's quickly replaced with a stoic expression. His eyes dart between me and the list as he contemplates his next move.

"I'm sorry, but you'll have to find someone else to help you." Jack pushes the letter back to me.

"Then I guess you'll have to find someone else to help *you* prepare for the meetings with the Wescott team." I fold my list and slip it back into my pocket.

"You're being unreasonable," he gripes.

"And you're being a grinch," I counter. "I suggested a fair solution, and you shut me down. You have no right to lash out considering you're not willing to give as much as you take. Now, if that's all, I need to leave for the airport to see if I can get on standby for the next flight to Maine."

When Jack doesn't reply, I turn to leave. I'm done letting him take advantage of me, consequences be damned. He'll have to find someone else to order around until January because it won't be me.

I'm nearly out the door when a hand wraps around my wrist, tugging me back. I look back to find Jack standing behind me with a conflicted expression.

"Ms. Stafford, please don't go. I apologize for overreacting." He says the words slowly, like they're painful to get out. "I don't usually celebrate the holidays, but I'm willing to make a concession and help you with your wishlist as long as I'm back in New York by the day after Christmas. I accept your conditions; do we have a deal?"

He extends his hand, and as much as I'm tempted to turn him down and give him a taste of his own medicine, I can't do it. This feels like the perfect opportunity to finally unravel the mystery that is Jack Sinclair.

"It's a deal." I shake his hand, solidifying our agreement.

Why do I have the feeling this arrangement is going to be far more complicated than either of us bargained for?

2

JACK

I WATCH PRESLEY CLIMB THE steps of my private jet. She's still in her workplace attire—a knee-length checkered skirt, white turtleneck, and black suede stiletto boots. Her brunette hair cascades down her back, and images of gripping it tightly while I plant a fiery kiss on her lips infiltrate my mind.

That's an inappropriate thought to have about my assistant.

There's no denying Presley is beautiful, but we work together. Not to mention, she's nine years younger than me. I've done everything in my power to maintain a strict professional relationship since hiring her, so I'm not sure why my dick is taking this particular moment to protest. It's probably because I haven't gotten laid in a while.

I've been working on multiple acquisitions over the last few months and rarely leave the office. It doesn't help that my entire staff wants to take time off during our busiest season. Hundreds of emails are waiting for a reply in my inbox, proposals that need to be drafted for three new clients, and multiple legal documents are ready for review. So why the hell am I putting it all on hold simply because my assistant said she had to travel home for the holidays? Or maybe the better question is why did I insist on going with her?

I attribute it to a temporary lapse in judgment. After seeing her holiday wishlist, there was no way I could let her go home to Aspen Grove alone, knowing that at any moment she could be kissing someone under the mistletoe.

"Mr. Sinclair, are you coming?" Presley asks from her spot at the boarding door.

"Yeah."

I jog up the steps to meet her. Once we're inside, I give a nod of approval to the flight attendant when she hands me a glass with two fingers of whiskey. I gulp the liquid in one swig, returning the empty glass to the tray.

The interior of my jet is furnished with eight leather seats to the left, two long couches to the right, and a large flat-screen TV built into the far wall. Presley leads us to the chairs in the back that have workstations, knowing that I plan to work the duration of the flight.

I'm aware that my employees have several choice nicknames for me, including hard ass, devil, and the Grinch. I'm a workaholic who keeps to himself and demands the best from my staff, and I make no apologies for that.

Most people assume that I inherited my wealth, but they're wrong. Sure, I grew up in an affluent household, with my father owning a successful pharmaceutical company and my mother coming from old oil money. Aside from paying for my education though, they haven't given me a cent since I graduated high school.

I didn't have a conventional childhood. My time spent with my father was reserved for being taught how to run a business and the importance of doing whatever it took to become successful. His version of tough love was cutting me off from my inheritance so I'd be forced to venture out and prove to him that I was capable of succeeding on my own. Still, no matter what I do, he'll never be pleased. When I earned my first million, he told me I wasn't working hard enough, and the day I became a billionaire, he was disappointed that I hadn't reached the status sooner.

"Why do you care so much about this holiday wishlist of yours?" I ask Presley.

I've been wondering ever since I came across last year's list.

"My mom goes all out at Christmas, and I guess you could say it's rubbed off on me. I usually have my family help me with my list. There's nothing better than spending quality time with the people I love and making memories that we can cherish forever."

I give her a curt nod, unable to speak past the lump in my throat. I distract myself by pulling out my laptop and firing off several emails.

I suppress a snicker when I open one from my mother's personal assistant with an attached generic "Season's Greetings" card. It's something you'd send a business associate, not your son, but it's befitting of our relationship— or lack thereof.

A part of me is envious of Presley, and I wonder if she knows just how lucky she is to have parents who care.

A black SUV is waiting for us when we land in Aspen Grove an hour later. Thankfully, there's an airfield right outside of town that's only a ten-minute drive to Presley's parents' house.

She insists the driver drop us off there and is planning to take me to the hotel once she's seen her family. I had her call earlier and book their last available suite, so I'll have plenty of privacy while I'm here.

I'm reading through a proposal from a new client when the car slows to a stop outside of a two-story Cape-style home with a wraparound porch. Thousands of colorful bulbs cover every inch of its exterior, and in the center of the yard are eight inflatable reindeer, complete with Santa Claus driving the sled behind them.

I roll my eyes at the dramatic display. I know she said her mom was obsessed with Christmas, but I'm not looking forward to spending the next few days with a bunch of Christmas fanatics. Why the hell did I agree to this?

Because it's better than spending the holidays alone in my penthouse.

At least I hope it is.

I wordlessly follow Presley up the driveway to the front door with our bags in tow, but almost run into her when she abruptly stops on the top step of the porch.

"What are you doing, Ms. Stafford?"

"You can't call me that here," she hisses.

I furrow my brow. "What am I supposed to call you?"

"Presley." Her tone is snarky. "Only my boss would call me Ms. Stafford, and you're not him, remember?"

"Fine. Why are we standing outside, *Presley?*"

"Um, I just realized I've never brought a man home before," she explains. "I always figured when I did it would be someone I was dating... Never mind, you wouldn't understand." She waves me off.

Before I can respond, the front door swings open and we're greeted by an older version of Presley—her mother, I presume. They share the same bright smile, ocean blue eyes, and straight brown hair. The older woman's hair is styled in a shoulder-length bob, and she's dressed in jeans and a Christmas sweater.

"You're finally here." She pulls Presley in for a bear hug. "I was so worried when you texted me to say that you missed your first flight. I should have known that grinch of a boss of yours would try and keep you from coming home."

"Mom," Presley warns.

"What? I mean it—the man is a tyrant. No reasonable person would make you come into the office at six a.m. every morning just so you can make him coffee before his first meeting. And then, as if that isn't enough, he makes you work fourteen-hour days, including Saturdays. You're a beautiful young woman living in the city and you deserve to live a life outside that office."

I have to suppress a scoff, failing to see the problem, considering Presley agreed to my terms before she was hired.

The firm's diverse portfolio includes several overseas clients, making early morning calls a necessity. Presley's an essential member of my team, and I want her on every client call. She's not only there to take notes; more often than not, she catches things other members of my team miss.

Plus, it doesn't hurt that she makes the best damn cup of coffee I've ever had. When she first started, I told her that I took my coffee black, but that didn't stop her from adding a splash of whichever specialty creamer was in season. I've never admitted it to her, but I've secretly grown to look forward to it.

"I've never met her boss, but from everything she's told me, he sounds like a goddamn nightmare." I can't stop myself from interjecting.

Presley spins around, staring daggers at me. A look of surprise passes her mom's face when she notices that I'm standing behind her daughter.

"Sweetheart, you didn't tell me you were bringing someone home."

"It was a last-minute decision," Presley grits out.

"I'm Jack. It's nice to meet you." I omit my last name just in case she would recognize it, considering her reaction to the mention of Presley's *grinch of a boss*.

"I'm Johanna," she replies. "And you are—"

"Presley's boyfriend." The lie falls effortlessly from my lips.

I like the sound of that.

Presley's jaw drops, her eyes widening in disbelief.

"Aren't you a little old to be dating a twenty-three-year-old?" The question comes from a guy who looks close to my age, stepping out of the house to hug Presley.

He's dressed in slacks, a white button-up, and a cobalt tie loosened around his neck. I'm assuming he just got back from a late night at the office which is something we have in common if he makes a habit of it like I do.

"Jack's thirty-two, the same age as you," Presley informs him.

"Which makes him far too old to be dating my baby sister."

"I'm Dylan Stafford." He extends his hand, giving me a firm handshake. "Mess with my sister"—he nods toward Presley—"and you'll be dealing with me and my brothers," he says in a threatening tone. "And just so we're clear, I don't make idle threats."

"I don't plan to—wait… Stafford… Maine… Brothers…" I mumble as the pieces fall into place. "You and your brothers manage Stafford Holdings."

"Yeah, we took over when our dad retired last year," Dylan replies. "Harrison is the CEO, Cash runs the operations side of the business, and I'm the CFO. And before you ask, yes, our parents did in fact name us after their favorite musicians." He smiles fondly at Johanna. "How do you know who we are?"

"Uh, I have a friend back in New York who's worked with your team before." It's not a total lie. I just don't mention that I've also done business with several subsidiaries of Stafford Holdings in the past. "Presley, why didn't you tell me your family owned the largest real estate firm in the country?"

I might be a billionaire, but my net worth pales in comparison to the Staffords. They have business holdings in every major city in the US, including hotels, office buildings, apartment complexes, and retail space. Their grandfather founded the company decades ago, and they've been expanding their business portfolio ever since.

I'm surprised I've never met the Stafford brothers in person, considering we run in the same circle. They have an office in New York City, but I wouldn't put it past Presley to have been making sure our paths didn't cross.

"I didn't want to be judged for who my family was." She shrugs. "I'd prefer to be known for my own accomplishments."

We have that in common. Although my parents forced me to venture out on my own whereas Presley chose to. I admire her gumption, but I'm still trying to wrap my head around the fact that she didn't tell me who her family was.

It's not like you asked.

I've never felt the need to get to know my employees. I pay them well to do their jobs, and before Presley came along, I didn't have an interest in any of their lives outside of work.

"Why don't we go inside where it's warm?" Johanna suggests.

I follow behind Presley as she steps into the foyer, taking in the welcoming space. A stairway leads to the second floor off to the left, and there's a living room on the right. Whites and grays dominate the space, creating a modern and calming ambiance. The open-concept floor plan makes the space feel roomy, but it's still a mid-sized home. I can't understand why the Staffords would live in a modest house when they could afford a mega-mansion—several, if they wanted.

"Aunt Presley, you're finally here!" A little girl comes barreling down the hall with a megawatt smile, her blonde curls bouncing as she races into Presley's open arms.

"Hey, Lola. I've missed you." The little girl giggles when Presley *boops* her on the nose. "Where's Gramps?" Presley asks.

"I'm right here." A middle-aged man comes down the hall, sporting worn blue jeans, a ratty T-shirt, and a baseball cap. "*Someone* was supposed to help me with the groceries but got excited when she heard her favorite aunt was here."

"I'm her only aunt, Dad."

"But you're still my favorite," Lola declares with gusto.

"Thanks, ladybug." Presley gives her another squeeze.

"I'm so glad you're home. We've missed you." Presley's dad gives her a kiss on the cheek.

"I missed you too."

"Aunt Presley, who's that man?" Lola asks loudly, pointing in my direction.

Great, the last thing I need is for her family to ask more questions.

Everyone looks at me, making me feel very uncomfortable. I'm usually adaptable in most situations, but I've never been caught in the middle of a family reunion before. I should have just had the car service drop Presley off and then take me straight to the hotel.

"That's Jack, her boyfriend," Dylan pipes up. "Jack, this is our dad, Mike." He grins with satisfaction when Mike throws me a disapproving look.

"Did you bring me a present?" Lola interrupts.

"Lola," Dylan chides. "What have I told you about asking people for gifts? It's not polite."

"But why?" She puts her hands on her hips. "Gigi says it's rude to show up at someone's house empty-handed." She grins at Johanna. "Does that mean this man is rude?"

Presley erupts in laughter. "Oh, sweetie, you have no idea." Her family gives her questioning glances. "Don't worry, Lola. Jack will get you a present. He just hasn't had a chance to go shopping yet."

"She doesn't need any more toys," Dylan interjects.

"Yes, I do, Daddy," Lola corrects him. "My Calico Critters need more friends. Jack can get me the panda family so they won't be lonely anymore."

I like this kid. She isn't afraid to ask for what she wants and has a counterargument for everything—she's definitely going places.

"Come on, ladybug. It's time to go home and get you to bed. It's been a long day." Dylan scoops her into his arms, and I notice he doesn't have a ring on. "See you guys tomorrow. And remember what I said about my sister, Jack. I'm watching you," he warns.

"Great," I mumble under my breath.

"Bye." Presley waves.

Johanna and Mike follow Dylan outside, leaving Presley and me alone.

"Where's Lola's mom?" I ask, wondering if she's still around or not.

"Maddie... she and Dylan met in high school. They dated for a while before getting pregnant with Lola, but motherhood didn't suit her. She left when Lola was only six weeks old. It's been five years, and she hasn't been back since," Presley says, seemingly surprised that I asked her something personal. I usually refrain from doing so.

"That's terrible."

"Yeah, it is," Presley agrees. "Dylan's a great dad though, and he has an incredible support system. A nanny comes in the mornings to take Lola to school, my parents pick her up in the afternoons, and she stays here until Dylan gets off work."

"Lola's lucky to be surrounded by so many people who love her," I murmur, unsure why I said it at all.

"Yeah." Presley gives me a quizzical look, but Johanna and Mike come back inside before she can ask about my cryptic remark.

"Dad, can I borrow the truck?" Presley asks. "It's getting late, and Jack needs to check in to his hotel."

"Don't be silly, sweetheart," Johanna chimes in. "He's staying with us."

"What?" Presley and her dad say at the same time.

"Your father and I weren't born yesterday. You're dating, so of course you share a bed sometimes. Your room is ready, and there should be enough towels in the bathroom for you both."

Fuck, I didn't think pretending to be Presley's boyfriend would backfire so soon.

"Uh, Jack and I both have meetings scheduled for tomorrow and Friday. We booked one of the conference rooms at the hotel, so it'll be easier if he stays there. Then I'll just meet him in the morning when my meetings are set to start," Presley offers.

She's doing her best to try and pretend I'm not her boss and that our meetings are not the *same* meetings, but I wonder how long we can get away with the lie.

"Nonsense. You can use your father's office. There's plenty of space, and that way, I can bring you lunch. I heard the hotel got a new chef last month and the food is terrible." Johanna turns to Presley's dad. "Don't you agree, Mike?"

"Agree with what?" he says through gritted teeth.

"You don't mind letting Jack and Presley use your office, do you?"

"No, of course not." His response is halfhearted.

He doesn't seem exactly thrilled about having a stranger use his office or sleep in the same bed as his little girl. I can't say that I blame him.

"Mom, really, it's no problem—"

"I insist," Johanna interrupts Presley. "You're staying here, and that's final."

"Fine." Presley sighs. "I guess we'll go up to bed then. It's been a long day, and we both have to be up early tomorrow."

"I can't believe Mr. Sinclair is making you work the rest of the week after he said you could have the time off," Johanna complains.

"It's only for the next two days, and then I'm off until the new year," Presley promises, glaring at me as if silently daring me to object. I don't.

"All right, sweetheart, I'll hold you to that. We'll see you in the morning." Johanna gives Presley a passing kiss on the cheek. "It was a pleasure to meet you, Jack." She pulls me in for a hug. "We're so glad you're here."

Things are about to get interesting.

3

PRESLEY

I STOMP UP THE TWO flights of stairs, Jack trailing behind with our suitcases.

My parents converted the attic into my own living area when I was in middle school so I could have space away from my brothers. However, the bedroom I used to think was spacious suddenly feels cramped when Jack steps inside.

"What is your problem?" I say through clenched teeth once he shuts the door. "Why the hell would you tell my mom you're my boyfriend?"

More importantly, why does the thought of dating Jack Sinclair send a flurry of butterflies through my stomach? I'm supposed to despise the man.

"I was worried what she might do if she found out I was your *tyrannical boss*," he deadpans. "At least that explains why you were adamant that we didn't tell anyone who I was."

I cringe at his tone. What did he expect? My mom is the first person I call when I'm having a hard day at work. I never thought she'd end up meeting the man responsible for causing me copious amounts of stress.

"If you weren't such a moody bastard, I wouldn't have anything to complain about," I quip.

"Well, I hate to break it to you, but you'd better get over your aversion to me real fast because we're about to get up close and personal." He motions to the full-size bed in the corner.

"Nope, not happening." I shake my head. "You got us into this mess, you can sleep on the floor."

I storm over to the bed and yank off the extra blankets neatly folded at the bottom, tossing them to the ground along with a pillow.

Jack should have thought about the consequences of his actions before he told my mom that we were together. I didn't miss her smile when she thought I finally had a boyfriend. Now, she won't be satisfied until I have a ring on my finger and she has another grandbaby on the way. She's going to be devastated when Jack and I conveniently "break up" after the holidays, and it's going to be all his fault.

"Immaturity doesn't suit you, Ms. Stafford. Why don't we handle this like grown-ups?"

"Ugh, you're so… annoying," I huff in frustration. "And for the last time, my name is Presley. You're supposed to be playing the part of my boyfriend, not conducting a board meeting."

"Okay, Presley." He drawls out my name. "In that case, I'm hurt that you would even suggest that we sleep apart. Didn't we agree to never go to bed angry?" he taunts.

"Oh my god, you're insufferable," I whisper-shout through gritted teeth. The last thing I want is for my parents to come upstairs to investigate the noise.

Jack and I have been here less than an hour and are already at each other's throat. Letting him come home with me was a colossal mistake, but there's nothing I can do about it tonight.

I grab my pajamas and my toiletries bag and rush to the bathroom, barricading myself inside. I put my things on the counter and look in the mirror, my reflection showing I'm a complete mess. Dark mascara streaks are smudged under my eyes, my hair is frizzy, and my lips are chapped.

"What am I going to do?" I mutter to myself.

This trip was supposed to be an uncomplicated and relaxing break from work, but it's turning out to be the opposite.

I go through my nighttime routine and change into my sleep shorts and tank top. If I had known while I was packing that Jack and I would be sharing a bed, I would have brought my oversized Christmas onesie or long-sleeved flannel pajamas. As it stands, my options are limited, and I don't want to raise any suspicions by asking my mom for something more modest.

Once I get the courage to leave the bathroom, I find Jack on the loveseat in the corner, typing on his phone. Is it too much to hope that he's planning an early exit?

Without a word, he goes into the bathroom, and I take it as my cue to climb into bed. I'm just dozing off when I hear the click of the door.

I glance up and my eyes nearly pop out of my head when I see Jack walking toward me in nothing but a pair of boxer briefs. No one told me he had the body of a Greek god under those three-piece suits of his. I can't seem to pull my gaze away from his sculpted washboard stomach, and I have the urge to trace every ridge of his defined abs. Thankfully, I come to my senses and realize that would be highly inappropriate given that he's my boss and I can't stand him.

Then why are you staring at him?

"Where are your clothes?" I demand.

"I'm sorry. I didn't have time to stop at home and grab my pajamas," he says flatly. "And this is how I sleep. You don't want your boyfriend to be uncomfortable, now do you?"

"I just assumed since you were the older, more mature adult in this situation that you'd choose to be the bigger person and let me have the bed."

"If sleeping next to me bothers you so much, you're welcome to take the floor." He points at the pile of bedding I threw down there earlier.

"Why do you have to be such a pain in the ass?" I hold my hand up when he opens his mouth. "Don't answer that; it was a rhetorical question."

I move to the edge of the bed, making sure there's a comfortable distance between us.

I tilt my head to look over at him. "You'd better stay on your side," I threaten.

"Don't worry; I will. The last thing I want is to get booted to the floor," he says with a wink.

He wouldn't listen when I told him to sleep on the ground the first time around. So I highly doubt he'd do it even if he did invade my space in his sleep.

"Good," I mutter. "Then we shouldn't have a problem."

I turn back toward the wall and pull the covers over my head. I hear the click of the lamp and Jack moving around to get comfortable. I have a feeling it's going to be a long night.

4

PRESLEY

I WAS RELIEVED THAT JACK'S side of the bed was empty when I woke up this morning. After getting ready, I went downstairs and found him talking to a client on the phone. We've spent the rest of the day in my dad's home office, hammering out the details for our virtual meetings with Mr. Wescott's team.

"Where's the finalized agenda for tomorrow? I asked you to email it out over an hour ago," Jack says, not bothering to glance up from his computer.

I wait to respond until he looks at me, ensuring I have his undivided attention. "Yes, but you also asked me to make dozens of changes to the PowerPoint you want attached to the email," I remind him. "I'm not a robot, Mr. Sinclair. I can only work so fast."

"How much longer is it going to take?"

I swear to god, he's the most impatient person I've ever met. "The more you interrupt me, the longer it'll take," I say in a snarky tone.

I get up from my makeshift desk in the corner, collecting the dirty dishes we used for lunch. Jack is getting on my last nerve, and I need some space before I lose my temper.

"Where are you going?" he demands.

"I'm taking a break. I can only tolerate your brutish behavior for so long," I answer honestly.

Without waiting for his response, I leave the room without a backward glance. I carry the dishes to the kitchen, and put them in the sink. I take a moment to regain my composure, leaning against the counter as I let out a heavy sigh.

Jack is testing my patience today, and the fact that we're stuck together for the holidays isn't helping matters.

"Are you okay, sweetheart?"

I spin around to find my mom standing in the doorway with a concerned expression on her face.

"Hey, Mom." I offer her a warm smile. "I'm fine. It's just been a stressful day at work preparing for some important meetings tomorrow."

"I'm sorry, sweetheart," she says with a frown. "I wish I could make things easier for you."

"It's okay," I assure her. "I'll have plenty of time to spend with the family after tomorrow."

"We're looking forward to it." She comes over to give me a hug. "I'm glad you brought Jack home with you. He seems like a nice young man. You deserve to be happy and have a life outside of your job."

I wouldn't necessarily describe Jack as a young man, especially not after seeing his six-pack last night. And he's most definitely not nice, but leave it to my mom to find the best in someone even as intolerable as him. I wonder if she'd still say those things if she knew who he really was.

"How do you know?" I teasingly challenge her. "You've spent all of five minutes with him since we got here last night."

"So? I'm a good judge of character, and I can sense that he has a good heart," she tells me. "It's obvious that he's completely smitten with you, and that brings me so much joy."

I suppress a humorless laugh. My mom's usually spot-on about reading people, but she's missed the mark with Jack. He's a self-centered jerk who most certainly doesn't have any interest in me. She must be blind to his true nature because she's excited that I finally brought someone home.

"I love you, Mom," I say, sidestepping her comment.

"I love you too, sweetheart."

"Listen, I have to get back to work, but I'll see you at dinner, all right?"

"Sounds good," she says with a soft smile.

It's late by the time Jack and I finish work for the day. After a quick dinner with my family, we head upstairs since we have an early morning ahead of us. I dread having to spend another night in the same bed as him.

"Someone's been very hostile today," Jack observes as he shuts the door behind him.

"Spending the day confined in an office with my temperamental boss put me in a rather cranky mood," I grumble.

"He sounds like a bastard. Want me to kick his ass?" Jack asks with a wink.

"Actually, yes, I could use some entertainment after the day I've just had," I tease.

I rather enjoy Jack's playful side, and I wish it surfaced more often.

"In all seriousness, we have a situation on our hands," he says.

"And what's that?" I ask with a hint of curiosity.

"We're supposed to be in love," he says matter-of-factly. "I don't think scowling at me at the dinner table qualifies as affection."

"Who said anything about love?" I mock. "Just because I brought home my *boyfriend* doesn't mean I'm in love."

"You don't strike me as someone who would bring a person home to meet your family if you didn't love them," he observes.

I've never been in a relationship long enough to entertain the idea of inviting anyone to Aspen Grove. That doesn't mean I haven't fantasized about it.

I hate to admit it, but Jack's right. I would never consider bringing a man home unless we were madly in love and in a committed relationship. I laugh at the irony that I did just that with my broody boss who also happens to be my fake boyfriend.

"It doesn't matter," I say, brushing him off. "If you weren't such a demanding boss, it would be easier to pretend that I like you."

His brows knit together as my response sinks in. Without a word, he sits on the end of the bed, gesturing for me to take a seat next to him.

I'm not sure what he's thinking, but it's clear there's something on his mind. I contemplate ignoring his request, but I don't think it'll do me any good, considering we're sharing a room. I hesitantly approach him, leaving plenty of space between us when I sit down.

A crooked smile tugs at his lips as he moves closer, erasing said distance between us. Butterflies flutter in my stomach, and warmth spreads across my cheeks when his leg brushes against mine. I've always found Jack attractive, but it's been overshadowed by the fact that I can barely tolerate him most days. I should push him away, but for some unexplained reason, I don't.

"I know I'm not an easy person to work for, and I apologize for being so difficult. I appreciate everything you do for me, and I should do a better job of showing it." His tone is remorseful. "I would really like it if we could get along, especially considering we're in such close quarters for the next few days." He gestures around my room. "What do you say, Presley? Give me the chance to make things right?"

My breath hitches when he places his hand over mine. Those damn butterflies in my stomach are now swarming, and it feels like my heart is going to beat out of my chest.

"That depends on if you're capable of acting like a civilized person rather than channeling your inner Jack Frost," I quip.

He chuckles at my jab. "I haven't heard that one before."

"Well, I think it suits you nicely," I taunt him. "If you haven't noticed, there are much better ways to getting what you want rather than acting like a tyrant."

He rubs his thumb against my hand, and the movement has me transfixed. What is wrong with me? Seconds ago, I was setting him straight, and now, I'm imagining what it would feel like to have his hand caressing my cheek while he kisses me. I rapidly shake my head to dispel the unwelcome thought.

I gently but firmly move his hand away from mine.

"I'm sure we can come to an agreement. However, I refuse to tolerate your brutish behavior any longer and expect you to treat me with respect moving forward," I say.

"Duly noted, Ms. Stafford," he acknowledges.

"Presley."

"What?"

"You're supposed to call me Presley, remember? Considering your status as my fake boyfriend and all."

"You're absolutely right, *Presley*. I won't make that mistake again."

I like the sound of my name rolling off his tongue. When he calls me Ms. Stafford, it's so stiff and formal, but when he says my first name it comes out warm and inviting.

"We have an early start tomorrow," I remind him. "We should get some rest."

These runaway thoughts of mine really need to be tamped down. Hopefully, my conflicting feelings will have disappeared by morning.

"Yeah, you're right," Jack agrees. "Why don't you go first?"

I give a small nod, excusing myself to get ready for bed.

We follow a similar routine as last night, and when Jack steps out of the bathroom, I can't resist sneaking a quick peek at him in his boxers. It's downright criminal for someone to be this attractive. When he turns to face me, I lie back on my pillow and snap my eyes shut, not wanting him to catch me ogling him. I hear him moving around for a moment before the mattress dips as he gets into bed, and I swear I can feel him looking at me. I cautiously open one eye, and sure enough, he's watching me intently.

"How do you expect me to sleep when you're staring at me like a creeper?"

"Need me to take the edge off, baby?" he taunts me with a smirk, clearly getting a kick out of provoking me. "An orgasm might help you fall asleep, and an attentive boyfriend would never leave you wanting."

I clench my thighs, doing my best to ignore the physical reaction his words have on my body.

"Oh my god, I can't believe you just said that." I turn to face the wall. "Goodnight, *boss*."

"Goodnight, Presley." His voice is low. "Sleep tight, beautiful."

I might have imagined that last part, but I don't dare ask.

We've been in meetings with Mr. Wescott's team all morning.

I'm having difficulty staying awake though given that I've spent the better part of the last two nights tossing and turning. It's been a while since I've shared a bed with a man, and I was petrified my subconscious would take it as a sign to cuddle with Jack in my sleep. Luckily, I've woken up to his side of the bed cold and empty both mornings we've been here.

"Can you repeat that?" Jack's grip on his pen is so tight that I expect it to snap at any second.

"We've covered all the time-sensitive items," Mr. Wescott says. "Let's reschedule the rest of the agenda until after the new year. It's the Friday before Christmas, and I'm giving my staff the rest of the day off." He smiles warmly at the camera.

"With all due respect, it's essential that our teams are prepared ahead of time for the changes coming in January."

"There's nothing that can't wait a few days." Mr. Wescott blatantly dismisses Jack's concerns. "When you get to be my age, you'll realize that work isn't nearly as important as it used to be. Everyone is burned out from the hundreds of hours we've spent preparing for this deal. We'll be much more productive once we've had a well-deserved break."

He has an excellent point.

I don't miss Jack's clenched jaw, telling me he doesn't agree, but it's obvious Mr. Wescott isn't going to back down on his stance.

"All right, Mr. Wescott. We'll do it your way," Jack releases a heavy sigh. "I'll have my assistant reschedule for the first week of January."

"Good. I'm glad we agree. Thanks for your hard work, everyone." He waves at the camera, and the call cuts off before Jack can get another word in.

"Well, that was a waste of time." He slams his laptop closed, running his fingers through his hair. "Schedule the jet to pick me up. I'm going back to the city tonight."

"You can't leave," I rush out. "I held up my end of our bargain. It's not my fault Mr. Wescott cut our work short. You're the one who had the brilliant idea to tell my mom we're dating, and she'll be devastated if you leave before Christmas. Besides, you can't go until you've helped me with my holiday wishlist."

Why am I trying to convince him to stay? Shouldn't I be happy that he wants to leave? However, I'm conflicted because something tells me that if he goes back to New York, he'll be alone over the holidays, which doesn't sit right with me.

"Fine," Jack mumbles. "I'll stay until Christmas, but not a day longer." He taps his fingers on the desk. "What's first on your list?"

"Ice skating," I say enthusiastically. "It's a family tradition."

"Why don't I sit this one out? I have work to catch up on, and something tells me you'll enjoy yourself far more if I'm not there, especially considering I've never been skating before."

"Don't be such a grinch. We can go early this afternoon so you can practice before my family gets there. Who knows? You might even end up having a little fun," I say, making me wonder if Jack even knows how to have a good time.

"Something tells me our definition of fun isn't the same," he grumbles.

"There's only one way to find out."

5

JACK

DESPITE THE SUN SHINING BRIGHT and the tune of "It's Beginning to Look a Lot Like Christmas" playing overhead, I'm not in a very festive mood.

I slowly inch around the outdoor rink, clinging to the wall for support. Presley didn't mention that ice skating would be so damn difficult. She tried to teach me, but after I snapped at her when I fell flat on my ass for the fifth time in a row, she left me behind, saying she refused to tolerate my surly attitude any longer. I don't blame her.

Everyone at the office tends to cower with fear when I enter a room, but not Presley. She's never been intimidated or afraid to call me out when she doesn't like something I've said or done. It's one of the reasons I consider her my best employee.

So why don't you start treating her like it?

I glance across the rink to find her gracefully skating across the ice. She's wearing a white pom-pom hat, her brunette locks falling in waves down her front and her eyes shining with excitement. Fuck, she's a goddamn vision and has completely consumed my thoughts since we got to Maine. Who am I kidding? She has dominated my thoughts every day for the past three years.

The last two nights have been torture, watching her parade around her bedroom in nothing but a tank top and shorts, revealing her long legs and generous curves. If I didn't know better, I'd think she was tempting me as payback. This morning, I woke up with a raging hard-on and resorted to taking a cold shower in an effort to control my reaction to having to sleep next to the woman who stars in my fantasies without being able to touch her.

Since we got to Aspen Grove, I've had to remind myself countless times that Presley Stafford is strictly off-limits, and even if she wasn't, she can't stand me.

It doesn't help that her family hasn't hesitated to vocalize how much they hate her boss. Thankfully, aside from dinner last night, I've avoided them for the most part, but now that Presley's in full holiday mode, something tells me that's about to change. I can't say I'm looking forward to meeting her other brothers, especially because I doubt they'll be any more welcoming than Dylan was.

"Jack, watch out," Presley squeals from behind.

I spin around to find her barreling toward me, her face filled with panic. I open my arms to catch her, but the force of the collision sends me sprawling backward. The impact knocks the wind out of me, and I grunt when I make contact with the ice.

"Oh shit," Presley cries out as she tumbles after me, landing awkwardly on my chest with a thud.

Once I've regained control of my breathing, I prop myself up on my elbow to make sure she's okay. Her head is nestled in my shoulder, and I start to worry something's wrong when she doesn't move.

"Presley, are you all right?" My voice is laced with concern.

I wrap my arm around her back, keeping her in place while I give her a once-over. Relief washes over me when she finally lifts her head.

"I'm fine," she says softly. "Thanks for breaking my fall."

"You're welcome."

The idea of her getting hurt sends a sharp pain through my chest. I instinctively draw her closer, comforted by the steady rhythm of her breathing.

Our faces are mere inches apart, and I'm captivated by how incredibly gorgeous she is. My pulse speeds up as I absentmindedly trace my finger along her jawline, silently counting the freckles scattered across her cheeks. She shivers at my touch but doesn't pull away. She shouldn't have this profound effect on me, but after years of denying it, being this close to her sends me over the edge.

There's a smudge of lipstick on the side of her mouth, and I gently wipe it off with the pad of my thumb. Her breath hitches in response, her plump lips practically begging to be kissed.

"Your hand is cold," she murmurs.

"Shit, sorry." I start to withdraw, but she surprises me by resting her palm against my hand, keeping it pressed firmly against her cheek.

"You should have worn gloves like I told you to," she chides.

"Since when do I ever listen?" I retort.

She tosses her head back, releasing a throaty laugh that's absolutely intoxicating. The world fades around us until my only focus is on the feel of having Presley in my arms. The tension is thick in the air as I'm met with her intense blue gaze. The desire to take things further is all-consuming.

"You have a thing for staring at me, don't you?" she says softly.

"Can you blame me when you're so goddamn beautiful?"

"You really shouldn't say things like that to me."

"Why the hell not?" I challenge.

"Because you're my boss," she reminds me with a hint of that sass I love so much.

Aside from our age difference, it's the only other reason I've kept my distance. She's always been off-limits, but in this moment, the fact that we work together doesn't seem to matter so much.

One kiss can't hurt, right?

I'm sure that thought will come back to haunt me later, but I couldn't care less right now.

I'm not thinking straight when I lean in to slant my mouth across hers, and our intermingled panting is music to my ears. I brush my lips against hers in a teasing stroke, and I am both shocked and pleased when she moans softly. I'm seconds away from giving this woman a proper kiss when a piercing voice from across the rink catches my attention.

"Presley, Jack, are you okay?"

I jerk my head up to find Johanna waving at us with a concerned expression. *Fuck.* I forgot Presley's family was meeting us, but now, I see the rest of them standing nearby. Her dad is glaring at me, Dylan's hands are clenched at his sides, and the two men who I assume are her other brothers, Harrison and Cash, look ready to beat me to a pulp.

I can't believe I almost kissed my assistant. In front of her family, no less.

What the hell was I thinking? I wasn't. That's the problem.

"You need to be more careful where you're going next time," I scold Presley like a total jackass, but I desperately need to put some distance between us before I do anything else reckless.

Her demeanor abruptly shifts from carefree to seething with anger.

"Geez, you don't have to be such a jerk." She scrambles to get up, shoving me back when I try to help. She storms off toward her mom, leaving me alone on the ice.

I scoot to the wall, grabbing the side, wobbling as I try to stand. I'm like a newborn calf trying to find my footing, keenly aware of everyone watching me.

I'm contemplating if it's possible to get off this rink without making a bigger fool of myself when Lola glides toward me like it's the easiest thing in the world.

"Want some help?" she chirps.

"Uh, sure. Thanks, kid." I hesitantly accept her small, outstretched hand and let her guide me to the exit.

"Daddy says you're Aunt Presley's boyfriend. Is that true?"

"Uh, yeah."

"She doesn't seem very happy. Did you make her mad?"

"Yeah. I said something I shouldn't have and hurt her feelings," I admit.

"Oh boy." She gives me a disapproving look. "I yelled at my friend Henry last week because he was playing with my favorite toy, and Daddy made me sit in time-out for five whole minutes. Is Aunt Presley going to make you sit in time-out too?"

I let out a chuckle. "I sure hope not, but I'll find a way to make it up to her, I promise."

"You could make her hot chocolate. That's what Gigi does whenever I'm upset." Lola's eyes light up.

"Thanks for the tip." I'm relieved when my feet are firmly back on solid ground. "I appreciate your help."

"Just remember," she says in a hushed tone, "I love Calico Critters, and I know for a fact that Santa isn't bringing me the panda family for Christmas."

"Good to know," I say.

Damn, this kid is persistent. Once Presley and I are back on speaking terms, I'll have to ask her to take me to the local toy shop so I can see these critters that Lola keeps talking about.

She grins at me before skating away. "Daddy, come skate with me," she hollers over her shoulder.

"I'm coming, ladybug." Dylan glares at me as he passes, not even bothering to say so much as hello.

"So you're the boyfriend, huh?" One of the guys who was next to Dylan approaches me. He's got shaggy brown hair, hazel eyes, and a jagged scar across his left cheek.

"Yeah, that's me."

"I'm Cash, Presley's favorite brother." He smirks. "Sounds like Lola's gotten to you too, huh?"

"Yeah, she's quite the little smooth talker. What'd she ask you for?" I'm curious if we're both being duped by a five-year-old.

"A giant giraffe stuffed animal. She says it'll fit perfectly in the corner of her room and will scare all the monsters away. She even said we could go in on it together," he says, pointing to his stoic brother standing next to him. "How thoughtful of her, right?" His tone is filled with amusement.

The serious one must be Harrison, Presley's oldest brother. His arms are folded across his chest, and his face remains in a permanent scowl. He's taller than his brothers, his black hair styled in a tapered fade, and he has the physique of a hockey player—lean and athletic. I'm used to being the most powerful person in the room, and even I'm intimidated by him.

"Do I know you?" he asks suspiciously.

"Nah, I don't think so." I shake my head, not wanting to imagine what he'll do if he finds out who I really am.

"You sure? You look familiar."

We've never met in person, but that doesn't mean he hasn't seen a picture of me somewhere. There are only so many billionaire CEOs in their thirties who live on the East Coast.

"Yeah, I guess I just have one of those faces," I try.

"If you say so." He sounds convinced but if his icy glare is any indication, he doesn't believe me.

"I'm going to go talk to Presley now," I say, preferring not to answer any more of Harrison's questions.

"It was good to meet you, Jack," Cash calls after me. "I'm sure Dylan's already warned you, but mess with our sister, and you'll be sorry."

I give him a curt nod, his subtle threat looming in the air as I walk away.

Johanna and Mike have joined Lola and Dylan on the skating rink, leaving Presley sitting alone on a nearby bench. She glares at me as I approach.

"Mind if I join you?"

She gives a noncommittal shrug. "You'll do what you want regardless, so it doesn't matter what I think."

"I'm sorry, Presley."

"For?"

"Being an ass. I had no right to get angry with you earlier. I'm just glad that you're okay."

"And…?" She impatiently taps her foot.

"If you're waiting for an apology for almost kissing you, you're not getting one."

"What? Why not?" She gapes in shock.

"Because. I'm. Not. Sorry." I lean in close, brushing my nose against her cheek. "If I remember correctly, kissing under the mistletoe is on your holiday wishlist, and I promised to help you check off *all* the items, did I not? If anything, I'm a man of my word. Let's call what happened on the ice a practice run."

Fuck. So much for keeping my distance. I might be playing with fire, but being this close to Presley does something to me that I can't explain, and I want more of it. I'm determined to get that mistletoe kiss, but will it be enough to satisfy my craving once I do?

"I hate to break it to you, but I took that item off my list before I asked for your help," Presley retorts.

"It doesn't matter. You wrote it down, which means it's fair game. Rules are rules," I tell her, keeping a stern expression even though we're discussing something seemingly juvenile.

"Says who?"

"Me." I stand up and reach out my hand. "Now, are we going to sit around and argue all afternoon, or are we going to skate with your family?"

"Go for it." She waves her hand toward the rink. "I'm sure Lola would love to teach you." She winks.

"Very funny," I say dryly. "The only person who's going to help me is you."

"Fine, but the next time you're a jerk, I'm leaving you alone on the ice and making sure there's no one around to save you."

"I'd expect nothing less, but I can assure you it won't happen again."

I wake up the following morning with Presley draped across my chest, her head nestled in the crook of my shoulder, her leg hitched up over my thigh, and her arm wrapped securely around my waist. My rigid cock is pressed against her stomach, straining against my boxer briefs.

She's climbed me like a tree in her sleep every night since we've been here. She doesn't realize she's doing it since I'm out of bed long before she wakes up, and I refuse to be banished to the floor if she finds out.

I slide out, careful not to wake her. I head straight for the bathroom, locking myself inside. If I were a better man, I'd take another cold shower, but I'm a selfish bastard. I strip out of my underwear, stepping under the stream of hot water.

My eyes fall shut, and I imagine Presley is here with me. I'd kneel in front of her, my hands gripping her thighs as I gazed up to find a wanton expression on her face while I brought her unbridled pleasure. I'd lick her pussy with my tongue, her fingers tangled in my hair as I worked her clit hard, telling her to be a good girl and come for me.

I let out a low groan, placing my hand against the wall for support, stroking my rock-hard cock with the other. I pick up my pace as visions of Presley crying out in ecstasy as she chases euphoria flash through my mind. My release hits me like a freight train, ropes of cum spurting to the ground.

Fuck.

I just crossed a line. I quickly rinse myself off, anxious to remove all evidence that I just jerked off ten feet away from Presley, in her parents' house, to images of their daughter coming on my face.

I'm relieved when I finish getting ready and find Presley still fast asleep. I head down to Mike's office, figuring I might as well get some work done before she wakes up and wants to do something festive.

The truth is, I actually had fun ice skating yesterday. It was nice to have an excuse to spend time with Presley outside the office, and I couldn't get enough of watching her infectious smile while she was skating with her family.

It's barely six a.m. on a weekend, so I'm surprised when I walk into the kitchen to find Johanna making blueberry muffins.

"Good morning, dear." She greets me with a warm smile.

"Morning. I didn't think anyone would be up this early."

"I figured I'd get a head start with such a busy weekend ahead. Those boys of mine are bottomless pits, so I like to have a few things on hand for them to snack on when they come over," she says fondly. "Why don't you sit down and I'll make you a cup of coffee while we wait for a fresh batch of muffins to come out of the oven?"

"Oh, um… I can get my own." I start toward the cabinet, but she holds out her hand.

"Don't be silly; I've got it. You sit," she orders.

I've already learned that it's pointless to argue with a Stafford, so I do as she said, taking a seat at the counter.

I watch with amusement as Johanna takes a Santa Claus mug from the cupboard and peppermint creamer from the fridge, not bothering to ask how I take my coffee. At least now, I know where Presley gets her affinity for seasonal creamers. Once Johanna's finished, she slides the piping hot cup of coffee in my direction.

"Thank you."

"My pleasure."

I take a small sip and let out a satisfied sigh. Like her daughter, Johanna has a gift for making the perfect cup of coffee.

"This is really good," I tell her.

I'm not used to having people do nice things for me, simply because they want to. Most of my time is spent with my employees who do things out of mere obligation, not because they have a choice.

"I'm happy you like it," Johanna says. "And I'm glad Presley brought you home."

"You are?"

"Of course. You seem like a nice guy, and it's about time she had a life outside the office. That damn boss of hers works her to the bone and never shows her any appreciation for all she does. She tries to downplay her stress, but I can hear the exhaustion in her voice every time she calls home." She pauses when the timer goes off and pulls out a batch of muffins that smell heavenly. "What kind of man makes his assistant work the week before Christmas when they asked for the time off a year in advance?"

A fucking asshole—that's who.

A twinge of guilt passes through me, knowing I'm the cause of Presley's undue stress. Instead of getting a much-needed break from work, she's been stuck with me twenty-four/seven for the past several days.

"If she's unhappy, why doesn't she quit? Couldn't she work for Stafford Holdings?"

"It's not from a lack of trying on her brothers' part. When she graduated high school, they begged her to join the team, but she insisted on venturing out on her own," Johanna tells me. "When she was six, we took her to visit New York City for the first time, and she's wanted to live in the Big Apple ever since." She laughs at the memory. "When Presley announced she was moving away, there wasn't anything we could do to convince her to stay. I don't care what she does as long as she feels fulfilled. All I've ever wanted is for my kids to be happy."

I can hear the genuine love in her voice, and it hurts to know that I haven't experienced that kind of devotion from my own mother and I probably never will.

"They're lucky to have you," I say with sincerity.

"You should tell them that." She spreads butter on a muffin—without asking, *again*—and sets it on a plate in front of me. "What about you? How many siblings do you have?"

"I'm an only child."

"Oh, I see. What about your parents? I'm sure they're disappointed that you're not home for the holidays."

Not likely.

I haven't spoken directly to my parents in… about three months. They were on a Mediterranean cruise the last time we talked and had plans to spend the month of December in Hawaii. I doubt they'll even bother to call me on Christmas, but I don't tell Johanna that, not wanting her pity.

"No, they're traveling." I keep my answer short.

"Well, you're always welcome here," she says, and I can tell she means it. Her genuineness makes me feel a little guilty for lying to her.

"I thought you'd be working."

I glance up to find Presley standing in the doorway of the kitchen. She's still in her sleepwear, a cable-knit sweater over the top, and red-and-green-striped fuzzy socks. Her hair is piled into a messy bun and she isn't wearing a stitch of makeup. Even first thing in the morning, she's still the most gorgeous woman I've ever seen.

"What's on the agenda for today, boss?" I ask playfully.

She gives me a menacing glare when her mom turns away.

"We're going to the Christmas market with my parents, and then we'll come back here to make gingerbread houses with my brothers and Lola."

"Sounds like a plan."

The Christmas market could be promising, but I'm not looking forward to hanging out with her brothers again. I'm pretty sure they'd rather watch me suffer in agony than let me spend another second with their little sister.

Sensing my foul mood, Presley stands behind me, draping her arms across my chest.

"Cheer up, Mr. Sinclair," she whispers in my ear. "That's two more items we'll be able to check off my list, making you that much closer to getting out of here."

I should be thrilled that I'll be back in New York soon, right? So why am I disappointed that my time out-of-office with Presley is running out?

6

PRESLEY

Aspen Grove's Main Street is bustling with people doing all their last-minute shopping.

A giant Christmas tree stands in the center of town, a beacon for holiday cheer. It's decorated with glistening lights, red and white ornaments, and tinsel. It's a long-standing tradition for the town's residents to decorate it the day after Thanksgiving, followed by a lighting ceremony. I have fond memories of participating every year growing up, but I've had to miss the festivities the last few years since living in New York. I make a mental note to start brainstorming ways I can convince Jack to give me time off next November so I can be here for it.

There's something magical about Aspen Grove this time of year. It's vastly different from the hustle and bustle of New York City. Here, you run into someone you know on every corner, and people aren't in a rush to get to their next destination.

The Christmas market is set up in the park across the street with dozens of merchants selling various goods, including homemade crafts, stocking stuffers, winter apparel, and ornaments. There are also several food vendors in attendance. A group of carolers near the entrance greets everyone with a cheerful version of "We Wish You a Merry Christmas."

We came with my parents, but they left to find the booth that sells gingerbread house–making supplies. Jack has been walking by my side since we arrived, silently taking in the festive atmosphere.

He might not talk about his personal life, but I've always suspected he has a strained relationship with his parents. Based on the amount of time he spends at the office and the sporadic emails from his mom's assistant. My suspicions were all but confirmed this morning after I overheard his conversation with my mom.

I'm not paying much attention to where we're going and nearly run into Jack when he comes to an abrupt stop. I look up to see a sign on the front of a booth that says, "Roasted Chestnuts for Sale."

He remembered?

I only showed him my wishlist one time, when we were in his office in New York. I haven't mentioned wanting to try a roasted chestnut since we got to Aspen Grove.

"We'll take one, please," Jack tells the vendor as he reaches for his wallet, but I place my hand on his.

"I can buy my own," I say.

"I know, but I want to do this." His tone doesn't leave room for argument.

This man is giving me a serious case of whiplash. One minute he's trying to kiss me, the next he's scolding me for bumping into him, and now he's insisting on buying me food. I'm not sure what to think.

"Thanks. It's the first year they've had these at the market. I've been looking forward to trying one ever since my mom told me this vendor would be here."

"Well, it's your lucky day," Jack says with a smile.

After he's paid, the cashier hands him a small paper cone filled to the brim with shelled roasted chestnuts. My mouth waters at the mere sight of them. Eager to taste one, I reach out to grab a chestnut but frown when Jack pulls the bag out of reach.

"Hey," I complain. "What are you doing?"

"Close your eyes." He takes a chestnut out of the paper cone and blows on it.

My eyes widen when I realize his intention. "You can't be serious."

"I've never been more serious in my life."

"Why should I do what you ask when you never listen to me?" I quip.

Considering he's been a constant thorn in my side for the past three years, I can't resist giving him a hard time. It's the least he deserves.

"You'll like this, I promise," he assures me.

I give him a wary glance. "How can you be so sure?"

"Because I know you better than you think I do," he answers honestly. "Now, close your eyes... please," he says, his tone softening at the end.

I nervously bite on my lip as I consider what he's asking. I can't believe I'm even thinking about obeying his request. Until a few days ago, he hasn't shown any interest in me. Yet his pleading expression has my resolve crumbling, and I'm taken back to our moment on the ice yesterday.

He was genuinely concerned when he thought I was hurt. I can still feel his hand cupping my cheek and the warmth of his lips brushing against mine. His moment of gentleness proved that beneath his gruff exterior, there's a thoughtful and considerate person, and I'll regret it if I don't give him a chance to show that side of himself.

"Fine." I hesitantly shut my eyes.

"Good girl. Now, take a deep breath for me."

My stomach flutters at him calling me a good girl. I shouldn't like how that sounds but I do.

"Now, take a deep breath and concentrate on the aromas in the air," he instructs.

I furrow my brows in confusion but don't argue. I inhale deeply and I'm instantly greeted with the scent of cinnamon, nutmeg, and a hint of smokiness. Combined, the smells bring back memories of baking with my mom as a kid and being cozied up by the fireplace with a cup of her homemade hot chocolate.

I part my lips when Jack presses the roasted chestnut to my mouth. I take a bite, chewing slowly, savoring the blend of nutty undertones and the subtle sweetness dancing on my tongue.

"What do you think?"

"It's delicious. You have to try one." I open my eyes to find him staring at me intently.

"Don't mind if I do."

I smack his hand away when he tries to grab another chestnut.

"Ow. What was that for?" He shakes out his hand in mock dramatics.

"You fed me, so it's only fair that I return the favor, don't you think?"

"If you insist," he says with a wicked grin.

I pluck a chestnut from the paper cone and hold it to his lips.

What the hell am I doing? This is not appropriate boss-employee behavior.

Like he can sense I'm about to retreat, Jack grabs my wrist to keep me in place. His liquid-amber gaze is trained on my lips as he guides my hand to his mouth. He eats the whole chestnut, leaning in to lick the lingering cinnamon sugar off my fingertips.

"You're right; it's absolutely delicious."

Holy shit, that was hot as hell.

I'm frozen in place, unsure how to respond as a spike of pleasure courses through my body, heat rushing to my core.

I panic when reality sets in. I just let my boss lick my fingers, and it turned me on. I jolt when it occurs to me that I want more from him... *so much more.*

I take a step back, worried about what I'll do if I don't put some distance between us.

"Um, we should go find my parents." I gesture in a random direction.

Oh my god, I'm making things worse.

"Sure," Jack says. "Let's go."

I follow behind, grateful he doesn't ask me to explain.

"What is that?" I gesture to Cash's so-called gingerbread house in mock horror. "It looks like a toddler made it."

It's a poor replica of a tiny home, haphazardly plastered together with white frosting. The roof is covered in chunks of icing, a failed attempt at making it look like snow.

"At least mine is still standing." Cash points to the caved-in gingerbread house that Dylan attempted to build. He tried to add a chimney, but the walls broke when he went to glue it on.

"Don't be sad, Daddy." Lola pats Dylan's shoulder. "You can help with mine. It's going to be so pretty."

"Thanks, ladybug." He presses a kiss to her forehead.

"That's cheating," Cash mumbles.

Since we were little, Mom insisted we learn how to make gingerbread houses from scratch. However, she's gone soft with Lola, buying her a kit from the store so it's easy for her to assemble. This year it came complete with colorful gumdrops, gummy bears, and hot pink frosting.

"Well, I think Presley should be disqualified," Dylan says.

"What? Why?" I exclaim.

"We were supposed to make a gingerbread house, not a gingerbread barn."

I ignore his jab, smiling proudly at my creation. I used red icing to cover the sides of the structure and decorated the top with black frosting to make it look like shingles. I borrowed some of the Little People farm animals my mom bought for Lola when she was a toddler, placing a chicken, a cow, and a pig near the barn doors that I made out of graham crackers.

"It's called using my imagination, Dylan. You should try it sometime," I quip. "We can't all be creative geniuses like Harrison."

We turn to watch as he adds the finishing touches to his two-story gingerbread mansion—complete with cutout windows and a layered almond roof dusted with coconut and icicles made of frosting.

Harrison has always been an overachiever. It comes with the territory of being the oldest and the successor to a global empire. While Dylan, Cash, and I felt free to explore our career options, Harrison saw things differently. Since he was ten, he knew that someday he'd step into the role as CEO of Stafford Holdings. He always had a choice, but he also felt like it was his duty to carry the weight of our family's burdens on his shoulders.

Since my dad retired and Harrison took over as CEO, his entire demeanor has changed. He never smiles anymore and is buried by his responsibilities. He and Jack are similar in that regard. They've allowed their circumstances to swallow them whole, making it difficult for them to find joy in the simple things.

"So, who's the winner?" Cash turns to my parents, who are standing nearby, observing our sibling banter.

"You know I can't choose a favorite, sweetie. I love them all." My mom claps her hands together. "They're all unique, just like each of you." She should have gone into politics. She's had plenty of practice keeping the peace while raising four kids. "Don't you agree that they're all perfect, Mike?"

"Yes, dear." He humors her. "But there is one I like better than the rest."

"Mike," my mom hisses.

My dad's been known to take sides in the past, which drives my mom up the wall.

"It's Lola's. You can't beat a pink gingerbread house."

My mother's face softens at that, accepting his answer because it wasn't one of us siblings.

"Yay," Lola exclaims. "We won, Daddy." She smiles up at Dylan. "Do I get a prize, Gigi?"

"How about a cup of hot cocoa with mini marshmallows?"

"Yes, please," Lola squeals.

"Great," Dylan mutters. "She's going to be up all night."

"I think everyone deserves a cup of hot cocoa. You're all winners in my book," my mom says.

"You hear that, Jack?" Until now, he's been silently watching from his seat at the table. "If you had participated, you could have had a cup of my mom's famous hot chocolate," I tease him.

"Don't listen to her, Jack." My mom fixes me with a scolding look. "I'll make some for you too."

"Hot cocoa for everyone." Lola waves her hands enthusiastically. She's holding a bag of icing in her hand, and we all watch as pink frosting flies through the air, landing in Dylan's hair. "Pink looks good on you, Daddy." She giggles.

We all burst out laughing—except for Jack. He's observing my family with an unreadable expression that I wish I could decipher. The sound of his phone ringing pierces the air, causing him to jump out of his chair.

"Excuse me, I have to take this." He abruptly leaves the room, heading for the front door.

"I hope we didn't scare him off," my mom says, concern lacing her tone.

"You didn't. He just doesn't like missing work calls since it could be a client."

"What exactly does he do again?" Harrison gives me a questioning look.

"He works in real estate." I keep my answer vague, perpetuating this lie a little bit longer.

"Huh, that's interesting, because it's a pretty small world when it comes to the New York real estate community. I know just about everyone, and I've never met Jack."

Damn it. Why didn't I say he worked in a different industry?

"Well, it must be bigger than you think," I hedge.

"Now, children, let's play nice," Cash suggests playfully.

Harrison's the smartest person I know, and if he's suspicious of us, then there's not much longer that Jack and I will be able to keep up this charade before our secret is exposed.

.

7

JACK

"YEAH, NO PROBLEM. YOU HAVE a happy New Year, too." I end the call, putting my phone in my pocket.

One of the reasons I've been successful in my business ventures is that I'm always accessible on short notice. It gives my clients and investors peace of mind to know that I'll pick up whenever they call.

During the time I've spent with Presley's brothers, I've noticed that they haven't taken a single business call when they're with their family. It makes me wonder if my priorities would shift if I had something—or *someone*—that I cared about to come home to.

I draw in a breath of fresh winter air. The setting sun casts a golden hue on the snow-covered ground as fresh snowflakes fall gently from the sky. The view is captivating, and I can admit that I've become very fond of Aspen Grove. Just like one of its former residents with entrancing ocean-blue eyes, chestnut brown hair, and a habit of putting me in my place.

"Everything okay out here?"

I turn around to find Presley in the doorway, worry etched across her face.

"Yes, I'm fine," I assure her. "A client had a pressing investment opportunity they wanted to run by me."

"Gotcha. I was beginning to think you'd just said you had a call so you could get out of there." She nods toward the house. "I know we can be pretty intense, especially when there's a gingerbread contest involved."

Presley's presence is all-consuming, and I take a step toward her, drawn to her like a moth to a flame.

"Yeah... to be honest, it's a tad overwhelming. I've never experienced anything like it before."

"What do you mean?"

As I see the sadness marring her features, I realize there's something about this woman that makes me want to confide in her.

"My parents weren't around much while I was growing up. Now that I'm an adult, I'm lucky if I hear from them every few months." I inhale deeply, considering my next words carefully. "We've never sat at the kitchen table for a meal together, let alone made any lasting holiday traditions as a family," I explain.

"I'm sorry to hear that," she says sympathetically. "I can only imagine how difficult it must be spending time with my chaotic family around the holidays."

"Your mom made me coffee this morning."

"Yeah, so? Is there something wrong with that?"

"No, of course not." I pause briefly. "It's just... she did it because she wanted to do something nice for me. Most people in my life only do things because they're obligated to—my parents included."

"I'm sorry, Jack. I know there's nothing I can say to fix things." Her tone is filled with genuine empathy. "I might be just your assistant, but I'm here to listen if you ever want to talk. You're not alone."

With a few choice words, she's somehow turned my world upside down. Regardless of how I've treated her or the number of shitty things I've said to her in the past, she's still willing to show me kindness.

"I never want to hear you talk about yourself that way again, do you hear me?" My voice is unwavering. "You're so much more than my assistant. Hell, you're more valuable than my entire senior executive team combined. There's a reason I want you on every client call. The company wouldn't be the same without you... I wouldn't be the same without you. I should have promoted you a long time ago."

"So why haven't you?" she asks, and I have to swallow the emotion welling up to tell her the truth.

"Because...I can't lose you."

She's been the only constant in my life these past three years. I might not always show it, but I look forward to seeing her smiling face every morning and to that first sip of coffee, guessing what flavor it'll be. The thought of losing Presley makes me feral.

"Oh..." She looks like she has something else to say, but stays silent.

"I shouldn't have crashed your holidays," I confess. "If I had known how much Christmastime meant to you, I never would have done it. It was wrong of me to put my priorities ahead of yours, and I'm sorry."

"Are you sick?" Presley rests her hand on my forehead.

"No?" It comes out as a question.

"You've apologized multiple times since we got to Aspen Grove, which isn't like you. The Mr. Sinclair I know would never admit he was wrong."

"It must be something in the air," I say playfully.

"Must be." She gives me a wry smile.

"I think I should go back to New York tomorrow. Christmas is only a few days away, and you should have a chance to celebrate without me here interfering. I'm sure your brothers will be more than happy to help you finish your holiday wishlist."

A wave of dread washes over me when I think about leaving Presley, but I'll go if she wants me to. It's the least I can do for the headache I've caused.

"You can't leave." Her voice is raised. "You promised that you'd stay until Christmas, and my mom would be devastated if you left even a minute before."

"Is she the only one who feels that way?" I close the remaining distance between us.

"Jack—"

"Well, I'll be damned," I interrupt when I spot mistletoe hanging from the doorframe.

When did that get there?

"What are you—" Presley's mouth shapes into an "O" when she follows my gaze upward. "My mom must have gotten it at the holiday market earlier."

"Well, that's convenient, seeing as how I owe you a kiss under the mistletoe and all."

"I really don't think that's a good—" She stops short when I capture her around the waist, pulling her against my chest.

"Remember what I said about checking off *every* item on your list? You wouldn't want to regret skipping one, now would you?" I taunt, unable to resist.

Presley hesitantly shakes her head.

"You deserve a magical kiss under the mistletoe, and I'm the one who's going to give it to you."

She's stiff as a board when I lean in to kiss along the edge of her jaw. Her breathing picks up when she turns to face me, and I take the opportunity to seal my mouth over hers in a possessive kiss. My tongue dances along the seam of her lips, coaxing her to let me in, and I groan with satisfaction when she opens her mouth to welcome me inside. Her invitation sends a coursing need flowing through my veins. Without a second thought, I lift her into my arms and she instinctively wraps her legs around my waist, her fingers gripping the nape of my neck. I take two steps forward so her back is pressed against the doorframe.

"Fuck, you're perfect, my little vixen," I say against her lips.

I didn't know kissing Presley would feel like this— passionate, intense, insatiable. Had I known, I never would have waited this long to have a taste.

She nips my bottom lip, moaning as she delves her tongue inside my mouth. She tastes like nirvana, and I can't get enough. My cock rubs against her core, and despite the clothing between us, I can feel the warmth of her pussy.

"Who left the door—"

Damn it, not again.

I jerk my head back to find Johanna standing in the hallway, a broad smile lighting up her face.

"Mom," Presley squeals with embarrassment.

She shoves at my chest, causing my grip to slip. She falls from my arms, thankfully landing on her feet, but a loud "umph" passes her lips when she hits the ground.

"Are you all right?" I ask.

"I'm fine," she clips, acting like we're high school kids getting caught making out for the first time. Based on Johanna's reaction, she doesn't mind what she walked in on one bit.

"Oh dear. I didn't mean to interrupt. I'm just going to go finish dinner. Close the front door when you're done." She heads down the hall without a second glance.

Presley's cheeks turn bright red as she buries her face in her hands. "Oh my god, I can't believe that just happened."

She doesn't give me a chance to respond, shoving past me to follow Johanna into the kitchen. I'm left standing alone under the mistletoe, wondering how far she would have let me go if her mom hadn't interrupted.

"I know you're awake."

I lean against the doorframe of Presley's childhood bedroom, watching her curled-up form move under the blankets. She shoots up in bed, leaning over to turn on the lamp. The soft glow reveals her staring daggers in my direction.

"I am now," she grumbles. "I don't know who wouldn't be considering how loudly you stomped up the stairs."

Presley ignored me for the rest of the evening after Johanna caught us on the porch. After dinner, she announced that she wasn't feeling well and went to bed early. Her mom invited me to play a game of charades, but I declined, instead excusing myself to Mike's office. I hoped that pouring myself into work would help take my mind off that searing hot kiss.

It didn't.

My raging erection is physical proof that Presley's all I can think about.

I waited until her brothers left for the night and her parents went to bed before coming up to her room. I had planned to sleep on the floor to avoid any more temptation, but now that she's here in front of me, my plans have changed. She's had enough space.

"Are you done avoiding me?"

"I'm not avoiding you." Her voice takes on a challenging tone.

"Oh, really? So, what do you call practically jumping out of my arms when your mom caught us making out or running away after that moment we had at the Christmas market?"

"You're one to talk," she fires back. "You literally shoved me away when my family showed up at the ice-skating rink the other day."

"I was scared," I admit.

"What could you possibly be scared of?" she asks, looking genuinely confused.

"You."

"Me?"

I slowly walk toward her, chuckling when she scoots up in the bed, her back hitting the headboard. There's no escape now—she's got nowhere else to go.

"You make me feel things I've never experienced before." I keep my voice low and steady. "If you haven't noticed, I'm insanely attracted to you, and now that I've felt your mouth on mine, I'm consumed with thoughts of kissing you again."

"This can't happen." She gestures between us. "You're my boss, and we both know if we take things any further, it'll only end in disaster."

A soft gasp escapes her mouth when I draw back the covers and join her in the bed.

"At the very least, you owe me another kiss, don't you think?"

"Too bad for you, there isn't any mis—" She stops short when I hold up the mistletoe I was concealing behind my back.

"You were saying?" She freezes as I brush a piece of hair from her face, tucking it behind her ear. "You're so damn beautiful, it's messing with my head," I utter quietly. "Tell me you're not attracted to me, and I'll stop. Say the word, Presley, and I'll walk away."

When she doesn't speak, I lean in to pepper several kisses along her collarbone. A soft moan passes her lips as I lick along her neck. I gently grab her jaw, rubbing my nose along her cheek, pausing when I get close to her mouth, silently encouraging her to reciprocate my advances.

When she sinks her slender fingers into my hair, it sparks a fuse inside me. I wrap my arm around her waist, tugging her into my lap to straddle me, and I plunge my tongue past her lips, ravishing her mouth with abandon. I don't stop until she's a blazing inferno of blissful agony, pleading for more.

I slip my hand inside her sleep shorts, teasing at her entrance.

"Fuck, baby. You're soaked for me."

She lifts her hips up as I shove two fingers inside her cunt, the crude sound of her arousal filling the room. It's sexy as hell as she shamelessly grinds against the palm of my hand.

"Oh god... Don't stop, Jack."

"You've got such a greedy little pussy, Presley."

She gasps when I plunge a third finger inside, increasing my pace.

"I need to come," she mewls.

"I'm not convinced." I keep my tone serious. "You want to come? You'll have to beg for it."

"Wh-what?" she stutters.

"You heard me, little vixen. Beg me like a good girl, and I'll let you come... eventually."

"You're so infuriating," she groans as I lightly tease her clit with my thumb.

"You like it," I taunt.

"Please let me come... Please, Jack," she chants as she plasters her body to mine, deliriously desperate to find a release that's just out of reach.

"I think you deserve a reward for begging so well, don't you?"

"Oh, yes, please."

I grab the bottom of her tank top, pulling it over her head and revealing her full breasts.

"What are you—"

"Damn, these tits are perfect," I interject.

I flick one of her nipples, grinning in satisfaction when it instantly hardens beneath my fingertips. I eagerly suck it into my mouth, biting down on the soft flesh.

"Fuck," Presley cries out.

I switch to her other breast, giving it the same treatment. Her moans of pleasure echo throughout the room as she welcomes the flash of pain I give with every bite to her nipples. She clings to me like I'm her lifeline, and I fucking love it. My hand is drenched with her arousal while I continue my assault, thrusting my thick fingers in and out of her cunt. She's burning with need as I bring her close to the edge again and again, pulling back just when she reaches the cusp of finding her release.

"Jack, please," she pants.

"What is it? What do you need?"

"Your cock. I need your cock."

I wasn't expecting that answer. Hell, I had no intentions of having sex with Presley tonight.

"I don't have a condom, baby."

"I'm on the pill, and I'm clean," she rushes out, her eyes aflame with lust.

"I haven't been with anyone since I was tested three months ago, and I always wear a condom." *Until now.* "Are you sure you want this? Because once I'm inside you, I won't be able to stop," I warn her.

She nods vehemently. "Yes, I'm sure."

Presley is going to be my undoing.

She transforms into a wanton vixen before my eyes. Her gaze is unwavering as she lifts off me to take off her sleep shorts and panties, tossing them to the ground. When she settles back on my lap, she effortlessly unfastens my pants. I let out a sharp hiss when she pulls out my erect shaft, guiding me to her entrance. She rubs the tip of my dick against her, in teasing strokes.

"Fuck me, Mr. Sinclair," she mewls. "Fuck me hard."

Her begging does me in.

"Gladly, Ms. Stafford."

I grip her waist, shoving her down onto my cock, pushing in to the hilt in a single thrust. Her cunt clenches around me at the intrusion and she grabs ahold of my shoulders, her nails digging into my skin as our intermingled groans fill the room.

"Holy shit. You're so goddamn tight."

I hold her steady as she bounces on my dick, arching her back with every thrust. She has me irrevocably under her spell, and I have no choice but to savor the feeling of being owned by this woman.

"Oh, yes," she cries out as she rides me.

"Damn, baby, you were made to take my cock." I slant my mouth across hers, kissing her fervently as I buck my hips in time with hers, picking up our pace.

"You ready to come?"

"I've been ready for forever," she whines.

I chuckle at her impatience, not giving her any warning before pinching her clit, sending her careening off the edge. I roar as unfiltered pleasure surges through me at the beautiful sight of Presley unraveling. I hold her tight as we ride out our orgasms together.

"Fuck, you're such a good girl, coming on my dick." I nuzzle my nose into her neck, inhaling her scent—a combination of vanilla and roses. I carefully lift her off me, not wanting to cause her pain. I stifle another groan as I watch our mixed cum drip down her thigh.

I slowly pull out of her.

"You're only going to fuck me once?" She pouts, teasing me with a glint in her eye.

It's adorable that she thinks I'm done with her. We won't be stopping until we're both boneless and sated.

"Have you ever had shower sex?"

She shakes her head.

"You're in for a treat." I smirk.

"Wait." Before I can move, she places her hand firmly on my chest. "This can't mean anything," she blurts out. "We're just having fun, right? Because I don't want this to complicate our working relationship."

How am I supposed to respond to that? What we just did felt like more than just *having fun*. That was an out-of-body experience for me, having Presley ride me as I worshipped her perfect body. Now that I've fucked her once, I have every intention of doing it as often as she'll let me. We've blurred the line between work and pleasure, at least in my book, and there's no going back now.

"Of course not." What's another lie added to the mix? "Let's get you in the shower. I can't wait another second to be buried inside that warm pussy of yours again."

Presley squeals with delight when I throw her over my shoulder, marching to the bathroom.

8

PRESLEY

I WAKE UP TO THE sun streaming through the window and a warm body wrapped around mine. I tilt my head back to find Jack sound asleep, his arms securely banded around my waist. My lips curve into a smile when I think back to last night.

Like he promised, we had sex in the shower—twice. We were still wet when he carried me back to bed, splaying me beneath him and driving me to the edge of insanity for what felt like hours before finally letting me come. The man may be considered a force to be reckoned with in the boardroom, but I learned last night that he's a total sex god in the bedroom.

Once we finally collapsed from exhaustion, he drew me to his side, where I fell asleep cradled in his arms—sated and content.

Thank god, my parents' room is on the other side of the house, because it would have been mortifying if they had overheard us.

I'm still not sure what came over me, begging Jack to fuck me the way I did. When I heard him coming up the stairs, I had every intention of ignoring him and pretending that our kiss under the mistletoe never happened. But then I saw him standing in the doorway, the epitome of sex appeal even dressed down in jeans and a T-shirt. When he pulled out that mistletoe, I was a goner.

It's like my attraction to him has been dormant all these years I've worked for him and my true desires are just now waking up. The more time we spend together outside of work, the stronger our connection becomes, but it's impossible to ignore the reality that there will eventually be repercussions for our actions.

Jack stirs behind me, and my skin erupts in goosebumps as his lips graze my neck.

"Good morning, beautiful."

"Good morning, Mr. Sinclair." I turn over to face him. "I'm surprised you're not up and working by now."

"I have a very good reason to stay in bed, wouldn't you agree?"

"Mmhmm," I murmur. "Although I'll admit I was surprised when I woke up in your arms. You don't strike me as a cuddler."

"I can only resist so long when a gorgeous woman is clinging to me like a baby koala."

"Come again?" I say with confusion.

"Every morning since we've been here, I've woken up with you practically lying on top of me." He chuckles softly.

"Oh my god." I cover my face with my hands. "Why didn't you tell me sooner?"

"Because you would have tried to get me to sleep on the floor, and that was never going to happen." He grabs my hands, peeling them away from my face. "If last night was any indication, it should be pretty clear that I don't mind."

"You're just saying that to make me feel better."

Jack pins me with a serious look. "Trust me, Ms. Stafford. I wouldn't have fucked you if I didn't thoroughly enjoy being close to you." He lightly traces my lips with his finger.

"Must you be so crass, Mr. Sinclair?"

"You wouldn't like me nearly as much if I were Mr. Nice Guy. You obviously have a thing for grumpier, older, wiser men," he says with a glint in his eye. "Me being your boss just adds a level of excitement to the mix."

This man may be a constant thorn in my side, but he's right. Something about him being my boss and being older makes him wickedly tempting and irresistible.

"Grumpier? Absolutely. Older? Yes. Wiser? Not a chance," I goad him. "Considering you had the ingenious idea of pretending to be my boyfriend."

Before I know what's happening, he flips me onto my back, leaving my head spinning.

"Oh, I think it was a brilliant move, considering our current position."

Jack climbs over me and I instinctively wrap my legs around his hips. He cups my cheeks, alternating between sucking on my upper lip and flicking his tongue across my mouth. He kisses me with enthusiasm, like he's starved, making me want to give him everything he asks for and so much more.

My smoldering desire bursts to life, setting me ablaze.

I entangle my fingers in Jack's hair. My moans reverberate through our kiss as his skilled tongue intertwines with mine, leaving me breathless and begging to be fucked again. Our intoxicating chemistry is maddening, and while my sole focus is on his hand sliding down my thigh, I almost miss the knock on the door.

"Presley, breakfast is ready. Are you coming down soon?" my mom calls from the hall.

"Thanks, Mom. We'll be right out," I squeak out, leaning against Jack's chest only once I hear her footsteps fade. "She has the worst timing."

"It's called motherly intuition," he teases. "Come on. We'd better get a move on before she sends your dad up here." He kisses my forehead and shoots me a playful wink.

"Seriously, these are the best pancakes I've ever had. Thanks, Mom."

I stuff another forkful in my mouth. One of the things I love most about my visits home is her exceptional cooking—it can't be beat.

"My pleasure, sweetheart."

I'm relieved she's acting normal, which means she either didn't hear anything when she came to my bedroom earlier or she's at least pretending that she didn't.

"Someone has a big appetite this morning… Any particular reason why that might be?" Dylan gives me a wary gaze.

IF YOU GIVE A GRUMP A HOLIDAY WISHLIST

He caught Jack and me kissing on the stairs on our way down to breakfast, which might explain his crabby mood.

"Nope. I just love Mom's cooking—that's all." I give him a smug smile. "Where's Dad and Lola?"

"He was shoveling the driveway when we got here, and she roped him into helping her make a snowman."

Sure enough, when I look out the floor-to-ceiling windows facing the backyard, I spot my dad pushing a giant snowball across the yard, Lola racing behind him with a carrot and top hat.

"Oh, gosh. Poor Lola," I say sympathetically. "Hasn't anyone told her that Dad is terrible at making snowmen? They always topple over before we have time to add the accessories."

"He tries his best, dear," my mom says from her place at the stove. "Why don't you go out and help once you've finished your breakfast? You can make sure that poor snowman stays upright."

"I'm planning on it." It might not be on my official holiday wishlist this year, but I'm definitely not passing up an opportunity to make new memories with my family.

And Jack.

"Dylan, where are your brothers?" my mom asks. "It's not like them to skip out on breakfast while Presley's in town."

"They had something they had to take care of this morning," he says cryptically.

"Make sure they know I expect everyone to be here tomorrow afternoon for our annual holiday movie marathon. Your father and I will be back by then."

My parents drive the three hours to Spring Haven to visit my aunt Clara for one night during the holidays every year to help her around her farm. I usually tag along, but I'm happy to stay behind this year, considering Jack and I will have the house to ourselves.

"Don't worry, Mom. We'll all be there," Dylan assures her. "What's on your agenda for the day?" He directs his question to me.

"Jack and I are going to stop by Winter Woodland. I spoke with Mrs. Taylor, and she said she was expecting a final shipment of balsam firs this morning."

Dylan knows I love being the one to pick out the tree that we all decorate on Christmas Eve. It's been a tradition since I was in middle school.

"Think you could do me a favor?" he asks.

"What is it?"

"I have some last-minute shopping I have to do. Would you mind watching Lola this afternoon instead?" He gives me a pleading look. "Jack can come with me, and we'll snag you the best tree on the lot while we're in town. We'll take my truck to load it up and bring it back here."

I've always loved the experience of going to pick out the tree, but I guess skipping out this year is okay, considering I'll be able to spend time with Lola.

"Yeah, that should work," I tell him before turning to face Jack. "As long as that's all right with you."

"That's fine."

His apprehensive expression doesn't convince me, but I offer him a smile in thanks anyway.

Dylan hasn't been particularly receptive to me bringing Jack home, so hopefully, they can get to know each other better while picking out the perfect Christmas tree. One can only hope.

9

JACK

"YOU'VE GOT TO BE KIDDING me," I grumble.

Dylan and I are standing outside Winter Woodland's empty tree lot, a giant "Sold Out" sign hanging from the chain-link fence.

"I don't get it. How could they sell out if they just got another delivery in? Presley said they always have plenty of trees to choose from."

"I don't know." Dylan shrugs. "They must not have had a good harvest this year."

"Should we drive to the next town over to see if they have any?"

"The closest city with a tree lot is sixty miles away. Besides, they get their trees from the same farm, so I guarantee they're sold out. There is another alternative," Dylan suggests. "Although I have to warn you, it'll require some serious manual labor and isn't for the faint of heart."

"What is it?" I ask, knowing how devastated Presley is going to be about not having a tree to decorate and wanting to make her smile.

"We can cut one down ourselves," Dylan says enthusiastically. "I know the perfect place we can find one. Harrison's dealing with business this afternoon, but Cash should be free. We'll stop by his place and pick him up. He's got an axe in his garage we can use."

My gut tells me this is a bad idea, but he wouldn't suggest it if it wasn't a solid plan. *Right?*

"Okay, sure. Let's do it."

I shove aside the nagging thought that I'm going to regret my decision.

"I'm not sure about this," I say skeptically. "We passed three *No Trespassing* signs on the way here."

"We're fine," Cash waves off my concerns.

We drove to the outskirts of town and down several miles of dirt road before finally pulling over. We walked around a bend in the road, where Dylan proceeded to inspect several trees.

The temperature has dipped as the sun's dropped below the horizon, and I rub my hands together to keep them warm. I should have listened to Presley and worn a warmer coat, but I didn't expect to be trekking around in the middle of nowhere.

"This is the one." Dylan waves to a medium-sized balsam fir. "It'll fit perfectly in Mom and Dad's living room. Don't you think, Cash?"

"Oh yeah, it's great," Cash replies enthusiastically.

"Don't we need a permit to cut it down?" I ask.

"Nah. We're friends with the owner. They won't mind," Cash replies.

"Are you sure?"

"Yeah, don't be such a worry wart."

"You do know that this is one of Presley's favorite holiday traditions… You don't want to let her down, do you?" Dylan prods.

"No, of course not."

Presley's done so much for me, the least I can do is get her this tree.

"You better get chopping before it gets dark." Dylan hands me an axe that I didn't notice he was holding until now, and then he and Cash start heading back toward the truck.

"Wait, where are you guys going?" I assumed they'd be the ones to cut it down since I've never done this before.

"We're going to bring the truck closer so we don't have to haul the tree so far."

"Okay…"

I stare at the tree in front of me, having no clue where to even start. I look back to ask if Cash can stay behind to help, but the brothers have already disappeared around the bend.

I grip the axe with both hands and take a swing, completely missing the tree and causing the blade to land in the snow.

This is harder than I thought it would be.

I tighten my grip before taking another swing that connects with the center of the tree trunk, the strike echoing through the forest.

I continue in a steady rhythm, wiping sweat from my brow after every few swings. I'm totally making Dylan switch with me when he gets back. He wasn't kidding when he said this would take some serious manual labor.

I'm probably about halfway through when I hear the distant wail of a siren, getting closer by the second. I pause mid-swing when a cop car comes barreling around the corner, parking a few feet away—its headlights aimed directly at me.

A tall, broad-shouldered man dressed in a sheriff's uniform exits the vehicle.

"What the hell are you doing?" he shouts as he storms toward me.

"Cutting down a Christmas tree…" I cringe at my confession. Maybe I should have withheld any information until I know what he wants. "Is there a problem, Officer?"

"So you admit you're chopping down a tree on private property? I assume you don't have a permit for that."

Shit.

I carelessly toss the axe to the ground. Not that it'll do me any good now.

"I'm here with the Stafford brothers," I inform him, assuming everyone knows them around here. "The owners gave us permission to chop down a tree since we couldn't get one in town."

At least that's what they told me, but now I'm starting to have doubts.

"Nice try," the sheriff grunts disapprovingly. "Everyone knows the city of Aspen Grove owns this property, and cutting down trees in this area is strictly prohibited. You're under arrest for trespassing and the destruction of property."

What the hell?

"Listen, why don't we wait until Dyl—"

"Show me your hands," he barks.

I swallow hard when I spot his holstered gun. It's probably best if I cooperate and we can get this sorted out once we get to the police station. I hold out my hands, and the sheriff doesn't hesitate to twist them behind my back. He cuffs my wrists tightly, the metal digging into my skin.

"Let's go." He motions toward his squad car.

Why the hell aren't Dylan and Cash back yet?

Without another word, the brooding sheriff drags me through the snow. Once we get to his car, he shoves me in the backseat and slams the door behind me. As he drives down the dirt road, I notice that Dylan's truck isn't in the same spot we parked it before.

When we make another turn, I spot the truck on the other side of the road. Dylan, Cash, and Harrison are casually leaning against the hood. I'm about to ask the sheriff to pull over when he tips his hat at them and they wave back, all turning to glare in my direction.

What the fuck? Where did Harrison come from?

I'm pretty sure those bastards just set me up.

"Rise and shine, princess," a low voice rumbles in my sleep.

"He looks like shit," another voice pipes up.

"A night in the slammer will do that to a person. It serves him right."

The last voice has me jackknifing to a sitting position, and I groan from the pain shooting through my joints. It wasn't a dream—I really spent the night in jail.

The uncooperative sheriff drove me to the police station in the center of town. There wasn't another person in sight as he dragged me through the building. He refused to let me make a phone call and left me in a holding cell without any food or water. I'm pretty sure he turned on the air conditioning too, because it felt like I slept in an icebox last night.

I scan the small room, stopping short when I see the Stafford brothers standing outside the jail cell. Harrison is grinning ear to ear as he leans against the bars, Dylan's casually sipping from a coffee cup, and Cash snickers while snapping photos of me.

"Will you cut that out?" Harrison says sharply.

"What?" Cash shrugs. "Trust me, these will come in handy if we ever want to blackmail him in the future." He gestures to his camera.

I knew this was a setup.

"Where's Presley? Does she know that you're harassing her boyfriend?" I growl.

"She's at our parents' house with Lola," Dylan says. "And cut the 'boyfriend' bullshit. We know who you really are, *Mr. Sinclair.*"

Oh fuck.

"I warned you not to mess with our sister." A sly smile passes his lips, clearly indicating that he thinks he's caught in some elaborate lie.

"You son of a bitch," I snarl. "You had no right to have me arrested and locked up in a dirty holding cell."

"Oh, we had every right." Harrison takes a step closer. "You've made Presley's life a living hell for the last three years," he states. "I knew there was something familiar about you, and a simple Google search confirmed that you were her boss. The question is, why the hell did you come home with her? And why would you pretend to be her boyfriend? Is tormenting her at work not enough?" His penetrating gaze is unyielding, and there's no way I'm getting out of here until he gets his answers.

"I needed her help with an acquisition my company finalized last week. When she refused to reschedule her trip, I suggested I come here with her instead. When we arrived and I heard how much your family disliked me, we agreed that I didn't need to share that I was her boss. So, when your mom asked who I was, it just slipped out that I was Presley's boyfriend. That's all there is to it."

"You lying bastard," Dylan shouts. "I saw you making out with her yesterday. Why would you take advantage of her like that? She's not a piece of property you can discard when you return to New York."

"I would never do that. She means too much to me."

"What the hell does that mean?" he demands.

"I'm not using your sister... I have feelings for her," I admit even though Dylan isn't someone I want to be having this conversation with.

"What kind of feelings?"

"All I can say is that your sister makes me crazy. From the first day she walked into my office, she's always been on my mind. Since we got to Aspen Grove, she's consumed my every thought, and I don't want things to go back to how they were before."

"Holy shit, you really do like her." Dylan sounds surprised.

"Yeah, I do. She's incredibly intelligent and not afraid to call me out when I'm being a pain in her ass. Plus, she's the most beautiful woman I've ever laid eyes on."

"We get it. You can spare us the sappy details." Cash wrinkles his nose in disgust.

The sound of creaking hinges fills the room as Harrison opens the cell door, gesturing for me to come out. "We'd better get going before the shift changes and people start asking questions."

"Wait, so I'm not being charged with anything?" I ask, confused about how they could pull this off.

"Nah. Landon and I played hockey together in high school, and he owed me a favor," Harrison says.

"Unbelievable," I complain. "Whose property were we really on?"

"Mine," he answers smugly.

You've got to be kidding me.

"Thanks to your little stunt, Presley still doesn't have a *real* tree to decorate, and tomorrow is Christmas Eve," I tell them, annoyed that their antics could interrupt Presley's holiday traditions.

"Don't sweat it." Dylan slaps me on the back. "I've got fifty balsam firs in my barn—you can have your pick."

"Wait… Did you—"

"Buy an entire lot of Christmas trees so you'd have to go out and chop one down yourself?" he cuts in. "I sure did. Not to mention, Mrs. Taylor made me cough up an additional two hundred bucks to play along."

"Damn." I'm pissed as hell, but I'm also glad Presley has brothers who have her back. "I feel sorry for the poor souls who ends up dating Lola when she's older. They're so screwed."

Dylan emits a low growl. "Lola isn't dating until she's thirty. Better yet, I'm going to convince her to join a convent and make a vow of celibacy."

"You let me know how that goes." I pat him on the back on my way out of the cell.

I'm anxious to get back to Presley.

10

PRESLEY

I BOLT UP FROM THE couch at the sound of the front door
swinging open.

They're back.

When I reach the hallway, my heart catches in my throat at
the sight of Jack stepping inside. His wrinkled clothes, messy
hair, and dark circles under his eyes do nothing to diminish his
sex appeal. Without thinking, I race into his arms, flinging my
arms around his neck.

"I've been worried sick," I tell him.

He gently lifts my chin, urging me to meet his gaze.

"I could get used to this kind of welcome." He chuckles,
pulling back from our embrace and pressing a kiss to my lips.
"I missed you, Presley."

I blink rapidly up at him, discerning whether his response
is authentic. He's not putting on a show because he's
pretending to be my boyfriend. I can tell that he genuinely

missed me, and I'm not sure how to reconcile that. This was supposed to be nothing more than a convenient arrangement, but it's quickly turned into so much more.

At least for me.

I tense up when I notice my brothers standing behind him.

"What happened last night? You were only supposed to be gone for a few hours."

While Harrison and Cash wear unreadable expressions, Dylan looks like a kid caught with his hand in the cookie jar. He's never had a good poker face, which always worked to my advantage when we were growing up and is working in my favor right now.

"It's a long story," Jack says.

"That's not an answer," I chide. "Did you really go to Dylan's house to watch football? He said you were having some male bonding time, whatever the hell that means." I add air quotes, letting them all know I know that's bullshit. "I was concerned when you didn't answer your phone."

Jack looks over at Dylan and lets out a roar of laughter.

I love that sound.

I can count on one hand the number of times I've heard Jack's genuine laugh, and all but one has been since we arrived in Aspen Grove. The first time was on my first day at Sinclair Group.

"What's so funny?" I ask curiously.

"Male bonding time? Really, Dylan, that's the best you could do?" Jack mocks. "Your brothers found out I was your boss and decided payback was in order."

Oh no.

I fix my brothers with an unyielding stare. "What. Did. You. Do?"

In high school, they were the masters of practical jokes, so the potential pranks they could have played on Jack are endless.

"We cleared out Winter Woodland's tree lot so Jack had to cut one down on private property," Dylan says.

If their past antics are anything to go by, I have a pretty good idea what happened next.

"Did you by chance force my boss to spend the night in jail?" I pinch the bridge of my nose, praying for patience.

"Yes!" Cash exclaims. "You want to see the photos?"

I can't believe this.

I turn to Harrison, who's been silent until now. "You're supposed to be the older, wiser brother. Where were you when this all went down?"

"Business," he states with a stoic expression.

"Business, my ass," I call him out. "I'm not stupid. This whole setup has you written all over it, especially considering the new sheriff is *your* friend."

"Why does it matter who was involved? The bastard had it coming." He gestures to Jack. "He lied to our family and took advantage of you. I won't tolerate anyone messing with my little sister, no matter who he is."

"Yeah, he deserved it," Cash chimes in.

"In our defense, we did warn him several times that there would be consequences if he hurt you," Dylan adds.

God, my brothers are idiots—protective, fiercely loyal *idiots*.

"You've got to be kidding me." I smack Dylan upside the head. "What is wrong with you guys? I'm a grown woman who can take care of myself. I don't need you interfering and acting like a bunch of teenagers," I complain.

"You're sexy as hell when you get all worked up," Jack whispers in my ear.

"Don't think you're off the hook," I tell him. "If you fire me over their little stunt, I'll have Cash release those photos so fast that you won't know what hit you."

I don't think he'd do that, especially considering we've slept together, but I doubt he's happy about my brothers having him arrested.

"Whoa." Jack holds up his hands in defense. "I'd never fire you, Presley. I might not like what your brothers did, but I'm glad you have them looking out for you. Besides, we're all good now, aren't we, guys?"

"I guess you're not so bad," Dylan grumbles. "But my warning stands. Mess with Presley again, and what happened last night will look like child's play."

"We're all good." Cash grins.

"Harrison?" I urge him.

"Yeah, whatever," he says noncommittally.

It'll have to do.

"I'm glad that's settled." I clap my hands. "Now, let's all agree that we're not going to mention this to Mom and Dad."

"Oh no." Harrison shakes his head. "You definitely have to tell them, but *after* Christmas. We're not ruining Mom's favorite holiday."

"Fine," I grumble. "I'll tell them *after* Christmas. Happy?"

The soft glow of the Christmas tree illuminates my parents' living room, making me smile every time I walk past it.

After the jail debacle was settled, I made bacon and eggs for breakfast while Dylan picked up one of the trees he confiscated from Winter Woodland's tree lot and brought it over. Lola and Jack helped me decorate our tree, and my brothers delivered the remaining ones to families in the area.

Yesterday, Mrs. Taylor had meticulously collected the names and addresses of everyone who had stopped to buy a tree after my brothers cleared the lot, promising they'd get theirs the next day, free of charge. She insisted Dylan would foot the bill for all the trouble he caused.

As promised, we were all waiting when my parents got home this afternoon to kick off our annual holiday movie marathon. My mom made her famous chili and another batch of hot chocolate while we made our way through *Elf*, *Polar Express*, and *Frosty the Snowman*.

Harrison and Cash left after the third movie to meet some friends at Old Mill, their favorite local brewery.

"Daddy, do we have to go home? Can't we stay and watch one more movie? Pretty please with a cherry on top." Lola flashes her best puppy-dog eyes.

"Nice try, ladybug," Dylan says. "It's already two hours past your bedtime." He holds his hand up, stopping her from arguing. "Tomorrow is Christmas Eve, remember? We're going to come over and make cookies with Gigi so we can leave some out for Santa Claus."

Lola's mood immediately shifts from gloomy to enthusiastic.

"Yay! Gigi, I can't wait!" She runs up to give my mom a big hug. "Can we make some extra cookies to take to Marlow?"

"Who's Marlow?" my mom asks.

"Our new neighbor." Lola beams. "She has bright yellow hair that looks like the sun, and her eyes are so cool—one is blue and the other green. She's so pretty. And Waffles came over to play with me the other day, which was so much fun." Lola bursts into a fit of giggles.

"Waffles is Marlow's dog," Dylan offers after Mom gives him a questioning look. "He dug a hole under our fence the other day, and now he sneaks over whenever he sees us out there. Lola thinks they're best friends."

"With who? Marlow or Waffles?" my mom teases.

"Both," Dylan complains.

He doesn't seem very happy about this latest development.

On the other hand, I can already see the wheels turning in Mom's head. Within a couple of days, she'll know more about Marlow than anyone else in town, including if she's single or not. Aside from the occasional one-night stand, Dylan hasn't been with anyone since Maddie left, and our mom has made it her mission ever since to play matchmaker. So far, her efforts have been unsuccessful, but something tells me she won't stop until Dylan has a new woman in his life.

"Let's go, Daddy." Lola jumps from the couch, practically dragging Dylan behind her.

"Coming, ladybug," he says. "See you guys tomorrow."

Jack and I are snuggled under a blanket, my head resting on his shoulder. *How the Grinch Stole Christmas* is playing in the background, but I'm finding it difficult to actually focus on the movie. We haven't had a moment alone today until now, and my mind is running wild with dirty thoughts about sleeping with my boss.

Jack's eyes are glued to the TV, but I'm keenly aware of his hand making its way up my thigh. He nuzzles his nose into the crook of my neck, inhaling deeply. "You smell so fucking sweet, like sugar, spice, and everything nice."

I gasp in surprise when he slips his hand inside my sweats. I'm glad I changed into something more comfortable—and conveniently more accessible—earlier.

"What if someone walks in?" I whisper.

It's unlikely since my brothers all left for the night and my parents went to bed an hour ago, but considering our track record, it's possible.

"Then they'd catch us watching a movie." He gestures toward the TV. "They'd be oblivious to the fact that my hand is buried inside your tight cunt."

"But it's not—"

He cuts me off by shoving his hand into my panties, and I let out a soundless gasp as he plunges three thick fingers inside me.

"Oh, god." I clutch the blanket, digging my nails into the fabric.

"You're fucking drenched." He lowers his mouth to my ear. "Have you been a naughty girl thinking about all the dirty things we did in your childhood bedroom the other night?"

I nod, so turned on that I can't find any words.

"You're such a greedy little thing." Jack smirks.

He pumps his fingers in and out in a steady rhythm while massaging my clit in languid circles. My body coils tighter with each thrust, a wave of euphoria washing over me. My sultry gaze connects with Jack's, and I grab his wrist, trying to control his pace, frantic for him to move faster. Unfortunately, my action has the opposite effect. The harder I writhe against his hand, the slower his movements become, until his hand finally goes completely still.

"Why did you stop?" I croak.

"Because I'm in charge of your pleasure tonight and I'll be the one to decide when you're ready to come, my little vixen."

He plants a scorching kiss on my lips to keep me from arguing and plunges his tongue in my mouth like he owns me—mind, body, and soul.

In this moment, I think he actually might.

He begins moving his fingers in short strokes, never going more than knuckle-deep. I don't miss his smug smile as I squirm against him, my body begging for release.

In need of a reprieve, I rest my head against the back of the couch. My eyes fall shut as I focus on my other senses. I listen to the quickening of Jack's breathing as he toys with me. The smell of my arousal fills the air, and I welcome the taste of cinnamon and bourbon as Jack brushes his tongue against mine. Just as I think I'm regaining some control, he thrusts his fingers deep inside me.

"Fuck," I moan loudly.

"It's mesmerizing to watch you lose control, baby." He speaks softly. "You're going to come for me now."

His order leaves no room for argument, and after a few strokes of my clit with his thumb, I detonate like a bomb. Tremors course through my body as my orgasm rips through me.

"You're such a good girl," he praises while stroking my hair. "I think my new favorite pastime is making you come."

My rapt attention stays focused on Jack's fingers as he brings them to his mouth, sucking them clean. He flashes me a wicked grin while he groans, like he's savoring a delicious treat.

"You're such an ass," I say teasingly.

"That's true, but that didn't stop you from coming around my fingers," he replies with a smirk.

I avert my gaze to the TV, not able to believe that really just happened. Jack gives a lighthearted chuckle as he shifts his attention forward.

As we go back to watching the movie, I see we're at the part where the Grinch's heart grows three sizes. It has me wondering if it could be possible for my grumpy, closed-off boss to have feelings for me.

11

JACK

THIS IS MY FAVORITE DREAM. Presley's full lips wrapped around my dick, her soft moans filling the room.

"Rise and shine, sleepyhead," she purrs in a sultry voice.

I furrow my brow, thinking that's odd. She doesn't usually speak in my sleep.

I don't think I'm dreaming.

My eyes fly open to find Presley positioned between my legs. She's stroking my shaft, her tongue twirling around the crown like she's licking an ice cream cone.

"Good morning, little vixen." My voice is still raspy from sleep. "You're a goddamn vision with your mouth on my cock."

She hums around my dick in response, lapping pre-cum from the tip. I wind my fingers through her hair, thrusting myself further into her mouth, and I grow stone-hard when her wet pussy brushes against my leg.

"Be a good girl and straddle my thigh so you can ride me, baby," I command.

She doesn't hesitate to obey, never taking her mouth off my cock. I push her head down, urging her on. I groan when she takes me to the back of her throat and cups my balls with her hand, squeezing lightly while sucking me off like a champ.

Fuck, she's going to be the death of me.

She unabashedly rides my leg while she blows me, angling her cunt so her clit rubs against my skin. Her high-pitched moans tell me she's already close to orgasm, and I'm right there with her.

"Presley, I'm going to come," I grunt.

I release her hair, giving her the chance to pull away, but when she shoots me a mischievous grin, I blow my load and watch in fascination as she eagerly laps up every drop. My cock springs free from her mouth with a loud pop when she's finished.

There's no doubt about it. Presley Stafford is my goddamn kryptonite.

"How come I don't get that kind of wake-up call every day?" I wink.

She bats her eyelashes, feigning an innocent expression. "Because I'm a professional, Mr. Sinclair. I don't mix business with pleasure."

"That's a damn shame."

"Why do you say that?"

"Because it's so much more fun this way."

To prove my point, I smash our lips together, and she yelps in surprise when I flip her over so she's lying flat on the bed.

"What are you doing?" she squeaks.

"I'm starving, baby. I want to finally get a taste of this perfect pussy."

I move to her apex, nipping at her inner thigh. When she tries to move, I hold her legs apart, pressing my nose against her core, inhaling her delicious scent. She arches her back against the bed as I lick along her seam from her pussy to her ass.

"Jack," she groans.

I don't hesitate to plunge my tongue inside her cunt, devouring her like she's my last meal. She throws her hands on my shoulders, chanting, "Yes," over and over, drowning in euphoria while I satisfy my appetite.

Damn, this must be what heaven feels like.

Presley's wet with her arousal, and this time, I don't make her wait long. I alternate between blowing soft puffs of air against her clit and pinching it firmly between my fingers, teasing her for only a moment before setting off her impending orgasm. Within seconds, her release erupts, and I bask in the taste of her against my tongue.

"Taste how delicious you are." I raise my head and mold my mouth to hers, groaning when she licks my lips. "You're such a good girl," I croon.

"You're a bad influence, Mr. Sinclair."

"Maybe, but something tells me you don't mind."

I caress her cheek, tracing her jaw with my fingertips as silence lingers between us. I wonder if she realizes that this is far more than just *having fun*, and if she hasn't, what it's going to take to get her there.

"Jack." Presley's soft voice breaks through my thoughts.

"Hmm?"

"Please don't go home until after Christmas." There's a hint of vulnerability in her voice that wasn't there before.

"Why would I leave? We haven't checked everything off your holiday wishlist yet," I tell her, feeling confident there's no way we got through the whole list in only a handful of days.

"Yes, we have," she says solemnly.

Presley leans over, grabbing a piece of paper from the nightstand. She unfolds it and hands it to me.

Presley's Holiday Wishlist

1. ~~Go ice skating~~
2. ~~Visit the local Christmas market~~
3. ~~Try a roasted chestnut~~
4. *Write a letter to Santa*
5. ~~Make a gingerbread house~~
6. ~~Holiday movie marathon + hot chocolate~~
7. ~~Decorate a real Christmas tree~~
8. ~~Kiss under the mistletoe~~

"What about write a letter to Santa? You haven't done that yet."

"I did." Her tone is somber. "Lola and I wrote our letters together while you were with my brothers."

"Oh."

Disappointment floods me when I realize she's right—that her list is complete. My stomach churns at the thought of leaving her and returning to New York. It's clear that things will never be the same between us… I just wish I knew what that meant for our future.

"Please tell me you won't leave yet," she says.

"I'm not going anywhere," I assure her. "I have to be here to give Lola her Christmas present, don't I?"

After speaking with Dylan, Presley and I visited Tinker Toys yesterday, and it's safe to say that Lola is getting everything she wants for Christmas.

Presley sighs in relief as she snuggles closer. "I'm glad you're staying."

Me too.

Johanna hands me a neatly wrapped box with a bright red bow.

"What's this?"

"It's for you. It's tradition for everyone to open this particular gift on Christmas Eve, and considering you're part of the family now, I didn't want to leave you out."

My hands tremble as I carefully open the gift, peeling back several layers of white tissue paper to reveal a set of red-and-black flannel pajamas and a pair of black slippers. I look around and notice that we all got the same thing.

"Mom gives us all matching pajamas every year," Presley says from her spot next to me on the couch.

"She shouldn't have gotten me a pair," I say quietly.

I feel guilty as hell, seeing as I'm an impostor. Johanna thinks that Presley and I are madly in love when, in reality, I coerced her daughter into bringing me home with her and then pretended to be dating her. Although it didn't feel much like pretending when I was balls deep inside her perfect cunt a few hours ago.

"Yes, she should have." Presley places her hand on my arm. "You wouldn't be here if I didn't want you to be," she reminds me.

"What about your brothers? Won't they be angry?"

I expect dirty looks from them all, but Harrison and Cash have left the room, and Dylan's helping Lola into her PJs, ignoring me altogether.

"I asked them earlier, and they said they're cool with it," she tells me. "You impressed them yesterday with your reaction to their prank. Harrison thought for sure you'd threaten to sue and storm out of here on your private jet."

I snicker. "If it were anyone else, I probably would have. However, I suspect I'd have done something similar if I had been in their shoes. You're an extraordinary woman, Presley Stafford, and you're lucky to have a family who would do anything for you."

"You're right; I really am." She gives me a soft smile.

I wish I could be a part of it for real.

"We should go get changed," Presley says.

"Yeah, okay."

She heads to her parents' bedroom and I use the bathroom down the hall. Once everyone returns to the living room dressed in our matching pajamas, Johanna claps her hands with joy.

"Let's get a quick picture," she says.

Everyone groans as she motions for her family to gather around the fireplace.

I think about moving to the other side of the room to make sure I'm not in the way, but I decide to stay in my place on the couch, staying outside the frame of their photo.

"You too, Jack," Johanna says.

"Oh, I don't think—"

"Come on, we don't have all day, Jack," Cash chimes in. "Besides, you in that outfit will make some great blackmail material."

When the Stafford siblings burst out laughing, Johanna and Mike give them curious glances.

"Inside joke." Presley shrugs, trying to play it off so her parents don't ask any questions.

Without further complaint, I scramble from the couch and hesitantly stand next to Presley.

"What are these for?" I ask when Presley's dad dumps a large pile of letters onto the coffee table.

"There's a special mailbox in the town center where kids can drop off their letters to Santa. Every year, our family collects them on Christmas Eve, and we read through them all."

"That's really neat."

"There are always a few kids who don't think Santa will visit them or who mention that their family is struggling financially. We can't help them all before Christmas, but from now through the new year, we anonymously drop off several care packages to families in need."

It warms my heart knowing that not only are the Staffords humble, but they also make giving back to their community a family affair.

"Oh no." Presley's face grows pale. "I promised Lola we'd drop her letter off to Santa's mailbox, but I totally forgot with everything else we had going on."

"Don't worry, sweetheart," Johanna says. "I took her to drop them off yesterday. She had two, so she must have forgotten to mention something she wanted in the first one."

"Definitely sounds like something Lola would do," Dylan says.

Presley lets out a sigh of relief. "Thanks, Mom."

I watch as each member of Presley's family grabs a letter and starts reading.

I hesitantly pick up a postcard with a handwritten note from a ten-year-old boy named James. He asked Santa for a skateboard and a king-sized bag of M&M'S. He said he'll know if Santa Claus is real or not depending on if he gets the candy he asked for since he hasn't mentioned it to his parents. I sure hope they read his postcard before he mailed it or they might end up having some serious explaining to do.

As we work our way through the giant pile, someone will occasionally share something they read if it's funny or heartwarming. We've also created a designated pile for those who might be in need of a Secret Santa.

There's only a handful of letters left when I pick up a bright red envelope with the word "Santa" scrawled on the front. I carefully open the envelope and unfold the single piece of paper inside. I'm greeted by familiar penmanship and pause when I scan the letter to find Presley's name in the signature.

Shit. I don't think Lola wrote two letters. She must have mistakenly delivered Presley's letter to Santa's mailbox too.

I should give it back to Presley, but something stops me. This might be the only chance I have to know what's going on inside that beautiful mind of hers, and I can't pass up the opportunity. I glance around, relieved to find everyone else immersed in reading other letters.

Dear Santa,

It might seem silly that a grown woman writes letters to a fictional man with a white beard who goes down people's chimneys to deliver gifts. This particular tradition has been a part of my yearly holiday wishlist since I was a kid, and I've never been able to let it go. It always gets me in a festive mood and helps me make new memories with the people I love most.

However, as I've gotten older, the spirit of the season has started to fade as I've been focused on going through the motions and doing things around Christmastime solely for the purpose of checking them off my list.

Everything changed this year when my grumpy boss hijacked my time off and came home with me for the holidays. If there were a real Naughty and Nice List, I always assumed he'd get nothing but coal. I thought him to be a jaded, broody asshole who only cared about himself, but I was wrong.

In a matter of days, Jack Sinclair has proven to be a kind and caring person, and dare I admit that he's quickly become one of the most important people in my life? He didn't just help me with my wishlist; he made sure that I enjoyed every minute while collecting new memories. He might not know it, but he's helped to bring back the magic of Christmas that I thought I lost.

He's going home to New York the day after Christmas, and I don't know how I'm going to watch him leave. Things have changed between us, and I can't go back to how they were before he came with me to Aspen Grove. I might have told him that what we're doing is just for fun, but the truth is that I'm falling for him. I'm not foolish enough to think that someone like Jack Sinclair could have real feelings for his assistant, but a girl can dream, right?

I've had this fantasy since high school that someday the man of my dreams would come home to spend the holidays with my family. Then, on Christmas morning, we'd get up before dawn and watch the sunrise from the ridge overlooking the lake at the back of my parents' property. Who knows? Maybe next year I'll finally be able to add it to my wishlist. Now, if only there was a reality where Jack was that man.

Forever a believer,

Presley Stafford

I stare down at the letter clutched in my hands.

How can Presley think she means so little to me? Not a day has passed since her interview three years ago that I haven't imagined what it would be like to have her in my arms. I wasn't willing to compromise her reputation by pursuing a relationship with her, so I've always kept my distance. Most days I'm lucky to get a few stolen glances around the office while she's taking notes or typing away on her computer.

To her, I've always come across as aloof and cold, because I was doing what it took to keep things strictly professional between us. In truth, I think I've been in love with Presley Stafford for the better part of three years, and I'm finally done pretending that I'm not.

She might not know it yet, but I'm going to make sure tomorrow is a Christmas she'll never forget.

12

PRESLEY

"TIME TO GET UP, BEAUTIFUL." Jack peppers kisses along my jawline while tenderly stroking my hair.

"Go away." I roll over, throwing a pillow on top of my face. "It's way too early. The sun isn't even up yet." I motion in the general direction of the window, my head still buried.

"It's Christmas morning, remember?" He lightly traces patterns along my neck while he patiently attempts to coax me from the comfort of the bed. "If you don't get up, I'm afraid your surprise will be ruined."

A surprise? For me?

That catches my attention, and I lift my pillow to peek over at him with one eye open. "What kind of surprise?"

He chuckles softly. "The kind that I can't tell you about unless you get dressed and come with me."

"This better be good," I mumble.

"Oh, trust me, it is," he promises. "Make sure to dress warm; we're going outside."

I give him a wary glance before climbing out of bed and changing into a pair of fleece-lined leggings, a thermal sweater, and wool socks.

The house is completely silent as we exit my bedroom and tiptoe down the two flights of creaky stairs. My brothers and Lola spent the night, and the last thing anyone wants is for Lola to wake up before sunrise, begging to open her presents.

When we get to the entryway, Jack stops me.

"What—"

He presses his finger to his lips, reminding me to be quiet, and holds out a black satin blindfold.

"Is that necessary?" I whisper.

"You don't want to ruin the surprise, do you?" he jokes.

"No, I guess not."

I comply with his request, turning around so he can tie the blindfold into place.

I'm not sure why I'm being so moody. He's only trying to do something nice, and all I've done since I woke up is complain.

I can't see a thing as Jack guides me to the front door, a cold breeze biting at my cheeks once we step outside. He holds me close as he leads me down the steps toward the driveway.

I can hear the faint sound of hooves clomping on the ground and low whinnies.

"What are horses doing here?"

"Nothing gets past you, does it?" He exhales. "We're taking a horse-drawn sleigh to where we're going. I think it's easiest if I lift you inside. Is that okay?"

I give a small nod, and he scoops me into his arms and climbs inside what I assume is the carriage. There must be someone else driving the sleigh, but I decide against asking any more questions to avoid ruining the surprise. Jack places me on a soft, cushioned seat and wraps a blanket around us, and I eagerly cuddle against his chest, rubbing my cheek against the warmth of his neck.

As the minutes pass, I become more excited about what he has in store. It's our last day together, and I'm grateful that we'll have some time alone to talk about where we go from here. I don't want him going back to New York until we've set expectations for what happens next.

When the sleigh finally comes to a stop, Jack effortlessly lifts me out of the carriage, setting my feet on the ground. He places his hand on the small of my back, his other clasped tightly in mine, as he guides me forward.

The sound of hooves clipping against the ground tells me whoever brought us here is leaving, which means Jack and I are officially alone.

"Can I take the blindfold off yet?"

"Not yet. Just a few more steps," he promises.

When he finally tugs off the blindfold, I blink rapidly as I adjust to my surroundings. It's still dark outside, but there's just enough light to determine that we're standing on the crest of the hill overlooking the lake on the edge of my parents' property. A steel firepit has been set up with a fire already crackling inside. Two chairs are positioned nearby, cushioned with fur blankets and pillows, and a wooden crate has been placed between them, holding a thermos and mugs.

"You planned all this?" I look up at him in awe.

I'm amazed that he would go out of his way to do something so special for me. I've always wanted to come to this place on Christmas morning to watch the sunrise, but until now, I didn't actually think it'd ever happen.

"I might have had some help," he admits. "I wanted to be sure that everything was perfect."

"It absolutely is," I say with appreciation. "Thank you, Jack." I wind my arms around his neck and tilt my head up to give him a kiss on the lips.

"My pleasure, beautiful," he says with a warm smile. "Why don't we sit down and enjoy the view?" He gestures toward the lake.

I take a seat on one of the chairs, snuggling into the cozy blankets. Jack sits next to me, twisting off the cap of the thermos, and pours a rich brown liquid into each of the cups before passing one to me.

"It's your mom's hot chocolate with hazelnut creamer," he says.

"Thank you." I take a sip of my drink, sighing in satisfaction. "It's delicious."

"It's the creamer," he quips.

We're cloaked in tranquil stillness. A blanket of fresh snow surrounds the lake ahead, the surface glistening like a field of diamonds. The first light of dawn appears over the horizon as the sun slowly rises, painting the sky in hues of rose, lavender, and gold. Birds begin to chirp, happily welcoming the new morning. It's a winter wonderland like I've never experienced before.

"The view is absolutely breathtaking. I can't believe I've never done this before."

"You're right about one thing," Jack says. "The view is unmatched. In fact, I dare say it's the most beautiful sight I've ever seen."

I'm prepared to tease him about getting sentimental over the scenery but am struck silent when I find his intoxicating honey-colored eyes fixed on me, the surrounding panorama the furthest thing from his mind.

A jolt of electricity shoots through my spine and I can feel my cheeks turning pink. All the while, Jack doesn't take his gaze off me as he leans in, gently tucking a piece of stray hair behind my ear.

"Coffee creamer reminds me of my mom." His smooth voice cuts through the silence. "French vanilla is her favorite, but I'm pretty sure she's tried every flavor in existence over the years. Every morning she'd come down to the kitchen while I was eating breakfast and prepare her cup of coffee. Whenever she'd try a new flavor, she'd let me have a sip. It was usually the only time of day that I had her full attention. Those moments might have been fleeting but I'm grateful for every single one." He pauses briefly before continuing, "Imagine my surprise when, two decades later, my new assistant brings me what I expect to be my preferred plain black coffee, and instead, I take a gulp of something that tastes like Dulce De Leche in a cup." He smiles at the memory. "I considered firing her for the inability to follow instructions."

I remember that moment like it was yesterday.

It was the only other time I'd ever heard him laugh outside of this past week. He took a long sip of his coffee, a surprised expression taking over his face. A burst of warm laughter escaped his throat, mesmerizing me. When he caught me staring, his demeanor turned on a dime, and he was quick to lecture me for not following his orders.

I ignored his request and kept making his coffee *my* way, hoping, one day, I'd be rewarded with another unfiltered laugh.

"Why didn't you fire her?" I continue playing along like we're talking about someone else.

"Because I was captivated by her brilliant ocean-blue eyes, fiery attitude, strong work ethic, and continued kindness, even when I was a constant pain in her ass." He reaches across to clasp my hands in his. "Presley, you should know that I wanted you from the moment you stepped into my office for the first time. I was tempted to throw you over my shoulder and take you to the nearest hotel. But after hearing how passionate you were about your career, I couldn't jeopardize that. Even though it meant I couldn't have you the way I wanted."

"And how is that?" I ask curiously.

"To be more than just your boss," he confesses. "I did everything I could to keep things strictly professional between us, but I couldn't bear the thought of not seeing you for two weeks. So, when I saw an opportunity to invite myself to come with you to Aspen Grove, I couldn't pass it up, consequences be damned. Plus, there was no way in hell I was going to give you the chance to find someone else to kiss you under the mistletoe." He flashes me a wicked grin. "Now that I've had a taste of what it's like to call you mine, I don't ever want to let you go."

"What are you saying?" I ask, my voice trembling.

"I'm in love with you, Presley Stafford."

I'm frozen in place as those three little unexpected words pass his lips. Love? *How is that possible?* Until the past week, we haven't spent time together outside the office.

"How can you be in love with me?" I blurt out, unable to hide my surprise at his declaration.

"You have captured my heart piece by piece, weaving your way into my very soul, and before I knew it, you had claimed all of me."

"I still don't understand. You never showed any interest in me until this past week, and you've always been cold, withdrawn, and demanding. I don't care *why* you treated me that way. I just care that you did." I take a shaky breath, forcing myself to keep going. "You admitted to never promoting me because you didn't want to lose me as your assistant. Which was solely for your benefit—not mine. How does that equate to love?"

Jack stands from his seat, running his fingers through his hair as he paces in the snow. "I know I've fucked up in the past by not treating you the way that I should have. But that doesn't change how I feel about you. Why do you have to be so damn difficult?"

"Me?" I raise my voice in frustration. "You're the one who's spouting crazy notions about love. The last time I checked, you were just pretending to be my boyfriend."

Until today, he hasn't said anything to indicate that he might want more than a casual fling.

"Let me make one thing clear." His voice is unwavering. "From the moment I kissed you for the first time, this has been real for me."—He motions between us—"there is nothing I want more than to be with you, and I thought you were falling for me too" he says, his tone laced with confusion.

"Of course I'm—" I cut myself off because I don't remember telling him I was falling for him. Taking in my surroundings and processing what he just said, I know exactly what's happened. I continue, my voice composed, "You read my letter."

How could he invade my privacy like that?

"Yeah, I did," he admits. "It turns out Lola didn't write two letters. She brought yours along when your mom took her to drop hers off in Santa's mailbox. I should have told you as soon as I found it, but I couldn't. I had to find out what's been going on in that mind of yours."

"If you wanted to know, you should have asked me." I set my cup of hot chocolate on the crate. "Who's to say that I wouldn't have chosen to pursue a relationship with you over working together if I had the chance? Or decided that I'd be happy to move to a different department so I could grow my career while also being with you? From day one, you've assumed that you knew what was best for me, which was wrong."

He presses his lips tightly together, apparently not pleased with my assessment. Why does he have to be so goddamn stubborn? If he would have opened up to me, we wouldn't be having this argument.

"I couldn't take the chance of losing you. I was concerned that I would scare you off if I said anything, especially considering there was no guarantee that you felt the same way that I did."

"That wasn't your call to make." I stand up, tossing my blanket on the chair. "This morning has been absolutely perfect, and I don't want to ruin the moment we've shared. I'm very angry with you right now, and if I stay, I'm going to say something I'll regret."

Jack nods in understanding before I turn away, heading in the direction of the house.

The truth is I have fallen hard for Jack Sinclair—the boss who's been a constant thorn in my side. I didn't fully realize the depths of my feelings until now.

I'm struggling to wrap my head around the possibility that he could love me, considering his actions over the years and the fact that we've only spent time together outside of work this past week. Despite that, the hopeless romantic within me clings to Jack's declaration like a lifeline. The question is, which side will come out on top?

13

JACK

IT'S LIKE MY HEART IS being ripped from my chest as I'm forced to watch Presley walk away. I'd chase after her if I thought it'd help, but it's clear she needs time to process what I told her. I don't blame her for wanting space.

Fuck.

This isn't how I imagined this morning going. I wanted to do something memorable to show how much she means to me. I didn't plan on dropping the L-bomb, but I got caught up in the moment while I watched her unfiltered reaction to the sunrise. She is the most captivating woman I've ever known and I couldn't stop myself from confessing my true feelings. But like always, I had to go and screw everything up.

I never should have read that damn letter.

I trudge the three miles back to the Staffords' place, unsure what to expect when I get there. As I finally round the corner to the front of the house, I spot Johanna sitting on the front porch with a worried look on her face. I climb the steps and sit down next to her.

"Did Presley make it back okay?" I ask.

"Yes, she did," Johanna confirms. "She didn't say much before going up to her room, just that you would be back soon. I take it things didn't go as planned?" She sounds disappointed.

I enlisted Johanna's help last night to help get everything set up for my surprise for Presley this morning. Although I did leave out the inspiration behind my romantic gesture, knowing she'd disapprove of me invading Presley's privacy by reading her letter.

"She loved the surprise," I assure Johanna. "However, I had to go and mess it up by saying something she wasn't ready to hear." My expression remains downcast. "I think I may have ruined Christmas for her," I confess.

"Don't be silly; you're being too hard on yourself," Johanna chides. "Every couple has arguments, and they don't always see eye to eye. Presley might be upset with you right now, but she'll come around once she's had time to think things through. There's nothing you can't get through together," she states confidently.

I'm not so sure about that.

Johanna has been nothing but warm and welcoming since I got here, but I wonder if she'll be so accommodating once I confess to lying about my identity.

"There's something I need to tell you." I nervously tap my foot against the step. "You've been so kind this past week and it means more than you know, but I've been withholding information from you that might change your mind about me…" *Here goes nothing.* "My full name is Jack Sinclair. I'm

Presley's tyrannical boss… The one she's always complaining about. I coerced her into letting me come home with her for the holidays when she refused to reschedule her trip, and it was my idea to tell you that we were dating."

Johanna's face is unreadable, and the lingering silence is grating on my nerves. I wish she'd say something… Anything, really. Even if it's to tell me to get lost and never set foot in Aspen Grove again.

"Jack, I know who you are." I'm confused when she gives me a warm smile. "I searched your name online the day my daughter told me she was going to work for you. I've never mentioned that to her so she must have assumed I didn't know what you looked like. So, imagine my shock when you of all people showed up on my porch and announced you were her boyfriend."

"Hold on." I rub my hand across my face. "You said all of those negative things about Presley's boss in front of me, even though you knew who I was?"

"Everything I said was true, wasn't it?" She shrugs unapologetically. "I was curious how you'd react to hearing those things about yourself."

"And?"

"You took it in stride," she admits. "From the minute you stepped on my porch, I could feel the chemistry brewing between you and Presley. I figured it was best to just let things run their course without my interfering."

That's bullshit, because that means she knew exactly what she was doing when she suggested Presley and I share a bedroom during our stay.

"So you don't mind that I want to date your daughter for real?"

"Over the past week, she's been happier than I've ever seen her, and that's because of you," Johanna says. "We've all done things we regret, and all we can do is learn, grow, and move forward. As far as I'm concerned, the past should stay in the past. There's no question you and Presley belong together."

"What if Presley disagrees?"

"You'll never know until you ask her," Johanna points out. "Besides, from what I'm told, Jack Sinclair *never* takes no for an answer," she says with a wink.

"You've got that right."

I knock on Presley's bedroom door, pushing it open when there's no answer. I cautiously step inside and spot her standing by the window overlooking the front yard.

"I saw you talking to my mom," she says.

"Yeah, she was waiting when I got back," I tell her. "She knows I'm your boss."

A look of disbelief crosses Presley's face. "You told her?" Her voice is raised.

"I did. It was wrong of me to withhold the truth in the first place, and I shouldn't have waited so long to admit it." I laugh softly while replaying my recent conversation with Johanna in my head.

"What's so funny?" Presley asks.

"Your mom knew who I was before I came to Aspen Grove," I inform her. "She searched for me online when you started working at Sinclair Group. Despite knowing the truth, she had you and me stay in the same room together this past week."

"Are you suggesting my mother set us up?"

"Indirectly, yes."

Presley shakes her head in disbelief. "Oh my god, I should have known she'd do something like that."

I owe Johanna for putting Presley and me in close quarters, giving me the courage I needed to transition our working relationship to a personal one. Now I just have to figure out how to fix what I've broken.

"For what it's worth, I really am sorry for reading that letter," I say with regret. "I should have talked to you about things from the start."

"You hurt me, Jack." Her voice is shaky.

She's absolutely right. I've caused her heartache and broken her trust. That pains me more than any physical wound ever could. However, that doesn't mean that I'm going to stand by and let her make false assumptions about our relationship.

"You're wrong," I tell her, needing to set the record straight.

"About what?"

"Me not loving you." I step toward her. My gaze is unwavering, making sure I have her undivided attention. "Could I have done things differently? Absolutely. I should have treated you better at work all these years—given you promotions, not demanded your time every second of every day, and made sure you knew how important you were to the company—to *me*. And I know it was wrong of me to read that letter without your permission. I might not be able to change the past, but I'm determined to do what it takes to prove how much you mean to me. Despite everything I've done, nothing has stopped me from falling irrevocably in love with you."

"You don't know me that well. How can you be in love with me?" she says with confusion.

How can she possibly think that I don't know her after all this time? I try to contain my smugness as I raise my chin and look her in the eyes, ready to prove her wrong.

"Your favorite color is lemonade pink—not magenta, not fuchsia, *lemonade*. You hate raw tomatoes, have an unhealthy obsession with seasonal coffee creamers, and you keep a jar of pink and red Starbursts in the top drawer of your desk. Every Tuesday, you wear your lucky black pencil skirt—the same one you wore to your job interview. And when you're nervous you play with the charm bracelet on your left wrist. You send all my employees generous birthday gifts and say they're from me, even though you use your own money because you think I'd say no if you asked me to pay for them. You've taken Gary the Doorman to lunch every Friday since his wife passed away last year. And despite your apartment being twenty minutes from the office, you walk to and from work because you like to immerse yourself in the sights and sounds of the city."

I close the remaining distance between us.

"I've spent the past three years paying attention to every last detail where you're concerned. Not out of obligation, but because you genuinely matter to me."

Tears spill down her cheeks, and I don't hesitate to wipe them away with my thumbs.

"I'll do anything to make you happy," I promise her. "If you want to leave Sinclair Group, I'll give you a glowing reference. Or if you want to move to another department, say the word and I'll arrange it. What I can't do is pretend this never happened." I motion between us. "What I feel for you is real, and I refuse to act like it doesn't mean anything when, in truth, it means everything."

"You invaded my privacy," she reminds me.

"I did," I acknowledge. "I'm sorry. I would take it back if I could."

"You've treated me with disrespect and acted like I was inconsequential to you."

"I know," I say with regret. "At the time, I thought I was doing the right thing by keeping my distance but I was wrong. I can assure you that will never happen again." I wrap my arm around her waist, drawing her closer so our mouths are only inches apart.

"You strong-armed your way into coming home with me and pretended to be my boyfriend."

"I have no regrets on that front," I reply with a smirk, trailing my fingers along her arm in teasing strokes, patiently waiting for her reply.

"I don't want to leave Sinclair Group," she assures me. "However, I would like to be considered for a transfer to the marketing department."

"Anything you want, baby."

"There's an opening for an entry-level associate position. I want to start there and work my way up. I don't want any special treatment just because we're dating."

"We're officially an item now, huh?" A smile tugs at my lips.

Please say yes.

"I should say no," she says honestly. "The logical thing would be to try to go back to how things were between us before and keep things strictly professional."

"But?" I encourage her to continue.

"But… I can't do that."

"Why is that, Presley?"

"Because I think I love you too." Her confession comes out as a whisper.

"Thank god, or I might have resorted to squatting outside your bedroom door until you agreed to forgive me."

"Watch your language, Mr. Sinclair," she scolds. "That's no way for a CEO to talk."

"Then it's a good thing we're not in the boardroom, isn't it?"

"It's a very good thing, because otherwise I wouldn't be able to do this." Her voice is smooth, like melted caramel.

She rises onto her tiptoes, slanting her mouth across mine. Her kiss starts soft and sweet, quickly transforming into an electric surge as she slips her tongue past my lips. Her lithe body is flush with mine, as she explores my mouth while she demands as much as she gives, providing us both what we crave.

"Jack," she mewls. "More. I want more."

"Easy, baby. I can't give you what you need with all these clothes on."

In record time, I strip out of my jacket, yank my shirt over my head, and tug off my sweats and boxers. Needing no encouragement from me, Presley follows suit, stripping out of her clothes, everything landing in a haphazard pile on the floor.

Left naked and wanting, she glances up at me, her vibrant ocean-blue eyes sizzling with lust.

If I had more patience, I'd take things slow. I would have started by stripping her clothes off piece by piece, laid her on the bed and kissed every inch of her body before making love to her.

But, no, there will be plenty of time for that later.

The need to be inside her is overwhelming, overriding any notion of going *slow*. However, that doesn't mean I can't have a little fun teasing her.

I grab Presley's hips, lifting her into my arms. She wraps her long, slender legs around my waist and encircles her arms around my neck. I walk back several steps until she's pressed against the wall. I waste no time, taking hold of my shaft and guiding it inside her cunt, inch by agonizing inch. It takes every ounce of willpower not to drive into her without inhibition, but I force myself to ease in gradually. Once I'm fully seated, I press a kiss to her forehead.

"Jack, move," she demands, wriggling against me.

"Someone's being a very naughty girl," I scold her. She mewls when I pull out, only leaving the tip inside her. "Good things come to those who wait."

I grit my teeth as I painstakingly fight against my primal instincts, pushing back inside her pussy little by little. She makes the most adorable high-pitched squeals as I do. Wanting to hear more of those sweet sounds, I suck one of her nipples into my mouth, alternating between biting and licking. She cries out in bliss as she digs her nails into my neck while I continue my onslaught of torturing her with pleasure.

"Shit. You're always wet...so fucking wet." My voice trembles as I try to maintain my composure. "Damn it, Presley, your tight little cunt has me losing all my self-control." I take a deep breath once I'm fully seated again.

It's a miracle I didn't shoot my load the second I entered her.

"Damn your self-control. I think you're trying to kill me," she quips.

"No, my little vixen. I just want to drive you wild. Is it working?"

"God, yes," she pants.

I pull out again and pause for a few seconds, letting her think I'm going to keep edging her along, before I slam into her tight cunt. She gasps in shock at the intrusion, her walls constricting around me, begging me to never leave. I lose all sense of control, my thrusts becoming frantic.

When she's on the cusp of release, I whisper in her ear, "Play with your clit like a good little girl." I lick along her collarbone while driving myself deeper.

She obeys, reaching between her legs and strumming her clit eagerly, clinging to my shoulder with her other hand. It fucking does me in, watching her get herself off while I'm buried inside her sweet pussy.

God, I can't believe Presley belongs to me. She has me completely under her spell, and I'll spend the rest of my life devoted to filling her life with happiness and joy.

"Jack." She utters my name with reverence.

"Ready to come, baby?"

She nods rapidly, gazing up at me and waiting for my permission.

"Come for me," I urge.

She shudders as her climax rips through her, my release taking over. I hold her close, peppering her face with kisses while she rides out her orgasm.

"I love you, Presley," I whisper in her ear.

"I love you, Jack. Merry Christmas."

"Merry Christmas, my little vixen."

Presley Stafford is officially, and forever, *mine*.

14

PRESLEY

MY PARENTS' LIVING ROOM IS covered with gifts, discarded wrapping paper, and ribbons. Christmas music plays quietly in the background.

Jack and I are curled up on the couch as he tenderly runs his fingers through my hair. I had no idea being with him like this could bring me so much peace.

"Lola, I think you missed a gift," Jack tells her.

She gives him a curious glance that morphs into a frown when she checks under the tree to find it empty.

"There's nothing there." She pouts.

"What about by the fireplace?" he suggests.

She spins around to find a pastel-pink-and-green package under the mantel. "There's another present, and it has my name on it!" Lola exclaims after further examination.

"It's from me and your aunt Presley," Jack says. "Why don't you open it?"

She eagerly tears off the bright wrapping paper and squeals with delight when she sees what's inside.

"It's the Calico Critters panda family. We're going to have so much fun together," she shrieks while cradling the box close to her chest.

"What do you say, Lola?" Dylan prompts her.

She carefully places her new toy on the ground before running over to the couch and jumping onto Jack's lap, wrapping her arms around his neck.

"Thank you, Jack. You're very helpful." She beams. "You're my new favorite."

"Excuse me?" Cash scoffs from across the room. "What about me and Uncle Harrison? I thought you loved your giraffe." He gestures to the giant stuffed animal in the far corner.

"You were my favorite yesterday." She giggles. "Jack is my favorite today, and Presley will be my favorite tomorrow."

"Aww. Thanks, Lola," I say with a smile.

"Since we're no longer your favorites, I guess that means you don't want to come outside and play with Uncle Harrison and me?" Cash calls out to Lola as he follows Harrison out the door.

"Wait, I want to play." She scrambles from the couch, chasing after him.

Dylan and my parents follow her outside, leaving Jack and me alone in the living room.

"I'm happy you're here," I whisper in his ear.

"There's nowhere else I'd rather be," he assures me, pressing a soft kiss to my hair.

After a late brunch, we gathered back in the living room to play games while eating hot chocolate and popcorn, followed by an afternoon nap for the whole family. Lola's not the only one who gets cranky when she's had an early start to the day.

Jack and I woke up first, so we decided to slip outside for a walk. We head into town, which is completely deserted while everyone is at home celebrating Christmas.

It's early evening, and the sunset casts a warm glow on Aspen Grove's Main Street. We stroll past the Bookloft, Tinker Toys, and the Bakehouse Bistro. I motion to the Brew Haven as we pass by.

"They make the best homemade coconut creamer." I wave to the store. "We'll have to stop by in the morning for coffee so you can try it."

"I thought we agreed that I could leave after today." He gives me a mischievous grin.

"You're welcome to leave anytime." I play along. "But that means you'll miss the nighttime parade tomorrow, featuring the Aspen Grove Singing Bears, and the annual after-Christmas fireworks show. Then, the day after that, we go to the matinee showing of whatever family-friendly movie is playing at the Sticky Shoe."

"You're right. I wouldn't want to miss out on the singing bears." He laughs. "Of course, I'm staying, but we're going back to New York on New Year's Eve."

"And why is that?"

"Because no one rings in the new year like New Yorkers, and I want you all to myself for a couple of days before we go back to work," he admits. "Plus, I can't wait to give you a New Year's kiss when the clock strikes midnight."

"How romantic."

"Did I mention there will be fucking? Lots and lots of fucking."

I burst out laughing. "Mr. Sinclair, we really need to work on that dirty mouth of yours." I plant a kiss on his cheek. "It wouldn't be a night spent together if there wasn't sex involved, now would it?"

"Glad we're on the same page," he remarks with a wink. "On New Year's Day morning, I'm taking you to Daylight Donuts on 14th Street. Their glazed donuts are to die for."

"No way." I shake my head. "The Donut Den on the Lower East Side has *the* most amazing glazed donuts."

"It sounds like we have a new tradition on our hands," Jack says.

"And what's that?" I ask.

"Spending New Year's Day trying all the glazed donuts in New York City to determine which one is the best."

"I like the sound of that." I lean my head against his shoulder. "Oh, that reminds me. I got you something."

I pull a white envelope from my coat pocket and hand it to him.

"Presley, you didn't have to get me anything," Jack says.

"I wanted to," I promise. "And something tells me you're going to love your gift."

He furrows his brow when he pulls out two tickets from the envelope. "VIP tickets to see the Sovereign Kings." His eyes widen with excitement. "Are you serious?"

"Sure am. I know you're a big fan. They're performing at Madison Square Garden on New Year's Day."

"How did you score these? The band rarely performs outside their Las Vegas residency at Premiere, and this show has been sold out for months." He holds out the tickets in awe.

"Stafford Holdings owns Premiere, and Harrison is good friends with its general manager, Randy Daniels. When he told Emerson—the band's manager—*the* Jack Sinclair wanted to come to a Sovereign Kings concert, he was more than happy to get us tickets."

"Wow. Presley, I can't thank you enough." He wraps his arm around me. "It's going to be such a tough decision to decide who to bring. Do you think Valentine would want to go? Or what about Sarah from accounting? I'm sure she's a Sovereign Kings fan." He grins widely.

I swat at him playfully. "You can take whoever you want, but there's only one person you can bring if you want to guarantee that you'll get laid after," I tease.

"Presley, will you go with me to the Sovereign Kings concert?" He dramatically clasps my hands in his. "Full disclosure: we're going to have lots of sex when we get back to the hotel."

"You are something else." I snicker. "But you're mine."

"And you're *mine*," he replies.

Yes, all his.

We make our way to the park next to the town Christmas tree. The ground is covered in a thick blanket of snow, and I can't resist turning around and falling back into the powdery white pile. I outstretch my arms and legs, moving them back and forth to make a snow angel.

"Jack, join me," I shout with glee.

He doesn't hesitate to drop into the snow beside me, and I fall silent as I watch him. There's no one else I'd rather spend Christmas Day with, and I'm still in disbelief that he's really mine. *Now and forever.*

"I love you, Jack," I murmur.

"I love you too, Presley."

I lean over, pressing my mouth to his, and he grasps my jaw, deepening the kiss. Our attempt at making snow angels is abandoned, the world around us disappearing. We're in our own private bubble, the outside world forgotten. We're two souls ignited by a mutual love for one another, and I can't wait for what our future holds.

My trip home to Aspen Grove didn't turn out how I had planned, but now I know what happens if I give a grump a holiday wish list...

He falls in love.

EPILOGUE

JACK

ONE YEAR LATER

THE PAST YEAR HAS BEEN A whirlwind, but has surpassed all my expectations.

When we got back to New York, Presley went straight to work on finding me a new assistant. After three months of seven failed trial runs and several heated arguments between Presley and me, which were followed by off-the-charts makeup sex in my office, we finally found the perfect fit. Mike's former assistant, June, moved to New York City last year to be closer to her kids and was searching for a new job. She fits in well at Sinclair Group and seamlessly took over the role of my assistant.

Presley transferred to the marketing department and has loved every minute of it. There are days I miss having her close by, especially when I'm craving one of her specialty coffee creamer concoctions. Thankfully, I was able to persuade her to move in with me in May, despite her initial concerns that we were moving too fast. I'm committed to this relationship for the long haul and didn't see any reason to wait.

I surprised her with a trip to Aspen Grove in November so she could participate in decorating the town Christmas tree and be there for the lighting ceremony. After going back to the city for a few weeks, we came out to spend Christmas with the Staffords. I've grown fond of Aspen Grove and look forward to our visits.

The smell of butter and vanilla fills the air as Johanna pulls out the last batch of sugar cookies. She's been bustling around the kitchen all day in preparation for a special Christmas dinner tomorrow and whipping up a variety of cookies to leave out for Santa tonight.

"Mom, it's time to open our presents," Cash hollers from down the hall.

"We better get a move on, Jack, or they'll start without us." She tugs off her apron, placing it on the counter.

"I'll be right there," I say.

I finish the last sip of my hot chocolate and rinse my cup out in the sink so Johanna doesn't have to worry about it later.

Presley's brothers took charge of getting matching pajamas for everyone this year. I've attempted to get them to spill the details, but even Dylan was tight-lipped about the surprise, meaning they've got something up their sleeve.

When I get to the living room, I sit next to Presley on the couch. Her hair is still damp from her shower, and I inhale the scent of vanilla and roses.

"There you are, beautiful." I intertwine her hand in mine. "I missed you."

"You saw me less than thirty minutes ago," she notes.

"Yes, and every minute without you felt like an hour."

"God, you're so cheesy." She laughs. "But I have to admit, I missed you too." She gives me an affectionate kiss.

After a morning of building an army of snowmen with her family, we spent the afternoon in her bedroom, doing things that involved fucking ... lots and lots of fucking. She tried coaxing me into taking a shower together afterward, but we never would have made it downstairs if I had joined her.

Lola runs over with two packages in hand. "Daddy says these are for you." She shoves one in my lap and gives the other to Presley.

"Thanks, ladybug." Presley gives her a warm smile. "Why don't you open yours first?" she suggests.

"Okay?" I say it as a question.

We should all be getting the same thing, unless her brothers decided to change things up this year.

I open the gift box and hesitantly pull back the tissue paper. I freeze when I see what's inside. The pajamas are custom-designed with pictures of me in a jail cell printed on the material.

This is one of the photos that Cash took.

Presley's brothers enter the room, all dressed in the same matching pajamas as mine.

"What do you think?" Cash grins. "Pretty great, right?" He gestures to himself.

"Oh my god, these are priceless." Presley laughs uncontrollably, tears streaming down her face.

I narrow my eyes at Cash. "You told me you deleted those photos months ago."

"I lied," he admits shamelessly.

"Wait. When were you in jail?" Mike growls at me.

Oh shit.

He might tolerate me because I'm dating Presley, but he's never been my biggest fan. He thinks I'm too old for his daughter and was livid when Johanna broke the news last year that I'm also Presley's boss.

"It was just a prank, Dad," Presley says, trying to defuse the situation. "Harrison, Dylan, and Cash thought it would be funny to have Jack arrested for chopping down a tree on Harrison's property."

Mike lets out a chuckle. "That's my boys," he says proudly.

I'm not surprised he'd side with his sons, considering their prank was directed at me. Here's hoping that when the time comes to ask for Presley's hand in marriage, I can persuade him to give his blessing.

The room falls silent when there's an unexpected knock at the door.

"Dylan, can you answer that?" Johanna asks with a glint in her eye.

She's up to something, and if it's what I suspect, Dylan won't be happy about it.

"Why me?" he complains.

"Don't worry; Mom, I can get it," Cash chimes in.

"No!" Johanna exclaims in a panic, reaching out to stop him. "Let Dylan do it."

"Okay, fine." Dylan sighs. "If it's that important to you, I'll answer the door." He gives Johanna a wary gaze as he crosses the room.

Anticipation fills the room as he swings open the front door to reveal a woman in her twenties. She's wearing a fluorescent-pink puffer jacket, a corduroy jumper, tights with a heart pattern, and white snow boots. Her golden-blonde hair falls in waves to her waist, framing her distinct, mismatched eyes—one blue, the other green.

This must be Marlow, Dylan's neighbor. I haven't met her, but Dylan complains about her any chance he gets. That hasn't stopped Johanna from trying to set them up. She mentioned a few days ago that she thought they'd make a cute couple, and I suggested that she invite Marlow over sometime during the holidays. It looks like she took my advice.

"Marlow?" Dylan utters with a hint of confusion. "What are you doing here?"

"It's nice to see you too, Dylan. Nice pajamas," she deadpans.

Dylan shoots her a hostile look, and she responds with a scowl. It's evident there's more to their mutual animosity than Waffles digging his way into Dylan's backyard or Marlow not shoveling her sidewalk every time it snows.

How could Johanna possibly think these two would be good together? Considering they're at each other's throat the second they're in the same space.

"Marlow, you came!" Lola squeals with delight. She dashes to the front door, wrapping her arms around Marlow's legs. "Where's Waffles?" She cranes her neck to look behind Marlow, hoping to see her four-legged friend.

"He had to stay home tonight," Marlow says.

"Oh." Lola's bottom lip starts to quiver, like she's on the verge of tears.

"Don't be sad, sweetie." Marlow crouches down so she's on Lola's level. "How about you stop by to visit him after Christmas? He helped me pick out your present, and I know he'll want to be there when you open it."

Lola's frown turns into a smile, and she throws her arms around Marlow's neck. "Oh goodie, I can't wait!"

"Waffles is just a dog," Dylan mumbles.

Marlow fixes him with an icy glare.

"No, Daddy, he's the cutest dog in the whole wide world, and I love him so much," Lola corrects him with a toothy grin.

"Yeah, Dylan, Waffles is *the* cutest, and deserves your respect." Marlow smirks.

This is even more entertaining than watching season ten of *Vanderpump Rules* with Presley.

"You never said why you were here," Dylan snaps at Marlow.

"I invited her," Johanna interjects from the living room. "Lola and I saw her in town the other day, and I told her to stop by for some cookies on Christmas Eve. Come inside before you catch a cold, dear." Her voice is warm and inviting.

I chuckle as Dylan hesitantly motions for Marlow to step into the entryway.

"Thank you, Dylan," Marlow says with mock sweetness.

He grits his teeth, struggling to control his temper.

Oblivious to the tension brewing, Lola grabs Marlow's hand, leading her into the living room with Dylan reluctantly following behind. He sits next to me, folding his arms across his chest like a sulking child.

"I can't believe my mom invited Marlow over," he mumbles.

"Oh, come on, she means well. Plus, she's been looking forward to this," I say with a chuckle.

"Hold up. You knew about this?" His voice is laced with irritation.

"Johanna might have mentioned that she thought Marlow was a nice girl, and I merely suggested she invite her over so the two of you could spend some time together. I didn't think she'd actually go through it." That's a lie. I knew Johanna would take action if I encouraged her.

"I can't believe you'd do that to me," he mutters.

"Payback's a bitch, isn't it?" I say with a smug expression.

If he hadn't been involved in orchestrating my "arrest" last year, I might not be enjoying his discomfort so much. However, given the circumstances, I have no regrets about how things have played out.

Presley swats my shoulder. "Watch your mouth, Mr. Sinclair," she scolds teasingly.

I lean in to brush my mouth against her ear. "You like it when I talk dirty," I whisper.

A shiver ripples through her, and I have half a mind to throw her over my shoulder and go upstairs, but I refrain. The last thing I want is to face Mike's wrath by keeping Presley away from her family tonight.

I turn my attention to Cash, who's in the middle of recounting a prank he pulled on Dylan back in high school that involved food color, and toothpaste. While the room erupts in laughter in response to something he said, a wave of nostalgia washes over me.

When I was a kid, I used to imagine what it would be like to be part of a close-knit family—one who gathered around the table for dinner, spent the holidays together, and openly gave their unconditional support. Now, after all these years, my wish has become a reality, and it's all because Presley has generously shared her family with me.

I was a shadow of a man, before she came along, living in solitude without a purpose beyond expanding my business ventures. She has breathed life into the darkest corners of my soul and awakened a passion for life that has long been dormant. She effortlessly fills the void that once echoed with loneliness, turning each moment together into a perfect blend of laughter, and shared dreams. Presley Stafford will forever hold my heart. I love her with all that I am, and will spend the rest of my days showing her just how much she means to me.

Want more Jack and Presley?
Type this link into your browser to read a bonus scene for *If You Give a Grump a Holiday Wishlist*:
https://bookhip.com/3vq8m0any3

Thank you for taking the time to read *If You Give a Grump a Holiday Wishlist*. If you enjoyed this book, please consider leaving a review on your preferred platform(s) of choice. It's the best compliment I can receive as an author, and it makes it easier for other readers to find my books.

ACKNOWLEDGMENTS

THERE ARE SO MANY PEOPLE who made this book possible, and I can't thank you all enough for your love, kindness, and support. *If You Give a Grump a Holiday Wishlist* wouldn't have been possible without each and every one of you.

To my readers—For rooting for me from the very beginning and motivating me to keep writing even on the days I think this might be all for nothing.

To my ARC team—Even before you saw the cover, read the book, or fell in love with Jack and Presley's holiday love story, you gave *If You Give a Grump a Holiday Wishlist* a chance. Thank you for all your thoughtful messages, posts, stories, reviews, and comments. Your endless love and support never ceases to amaze me.

To Sandea—For pushing me to follow my dreams even when I've been seconds away from throwing in the towel. You're my constant, answering my calls day or night, and are always there as a sounding board when I need it most.

To Caroline, Jovana, and Brooke—I couldn't ask for a better editing team. I'm grateful for your expertise and for pushing me to write a holiday novella worth reading.

To Morgan Elizabeth—Thank you for your friendship and for always being willing to answer my endless questions.

ANN EINERSON

To Ashleigh, Emily, and Jess—For being wonderful friends, collaborators, and cheerleaders. You make the day-to-day of being a writer so much more fun and far less lonely.

To Becca—Thank you for your invaluable advice and feedback. Without you, Jack and Presley's story would never have made it onto paper. I look forward to our plotting sessions and am forever grateful for you.

To Sarah—For literally designing the most adorable holiday cover of all time. I was obsessed from day one and it makes my heart so happy that my readers love it just as much as I do.

To Bryanna, Lauren Brooke, Tabitha, Cassidy, Meghan, Jenna Lynn, Claire, and Diana—Your honest, detailed, and candid feedback drove me to create the best possible version of this book. Thank you!

To Roxan and Randy—You taught me to believe in myself and to chase my dreams, no matter the cost. I love you both, always.

To Kyler—Thank you for supporting my insane work schedule, for tolerating the endless amounts of takeout and piles of laundry that accrued in the months leading up to this book's launch, and for helping to make my dream of becoming a full-time author come true.

ABOUT THE AUTHOR

ANN EINERSON IS THE AUTHOR of imperfect love stories that will keep you invested until the very last page.

Ann writes stubborn heroines who aren't afraid to put their moody men in their place. Each of Ann's books features a found family, an ode to her love of travel, and serves plenty of angst and spice. Her novels are inspired by the ample supply of sticky notes she always has on hand to jot down the stories that live rent-free in her mind.

When she's not writing, Ann enjoys spoiling her chatty pet chickens, listening to her dysfunctional playlists, and going for late-night runs on the treadmill. She lives in Michigan with her husband.

KEEP IN TOUCH WITH ANN EINERSON

Website: www.anneinerson.com

Newsletter: www.anneinerson.com/newsletter-signup

Instagram: www.instagram.com/authoranneinerson

TikTok: www.tiktok.com/@authoranneinerson

Amazon: www.amazon.com/author/anneinerson

Goodreads:
www.goodreads.com/author/show/29752171.Ann_Einerson

ALSO BY ANN EINERSON

STANDALONES

Forgive or Forget Me
The Spotlight